"Mesmerizing . . . Simultaneously visceral and breathless, this is one knockout of a novel." —*Booklist* (starred review)

"Magnificent . . . Sahota brilliantly plays with access to knowledge, to history. . . . [A read] that promises to haunt and illuminate." —*Shelf Awareness*

"*China Room* burns quietly but fiercely from first page to last—a gorgeous, gripping read." —Kamila Shamsie, author of *Home Fire*

"Boisterous, emotional, and heartrending, *China Room* juggles questions of love, debt, and what it means to build a home alongside the history that carries us. Sahota navigates the worlds between where we believe we belong, where we end up, and the choices we make to close the distance along the way, with humanity, precision, and grace—*China Room* is a propulsive dream, intricately wrought, and Sahota is a maestro." —Bryan Washington, author of *Memorial*

"*China Room* is a stunning novel, I'm blown away by it. It's so complex and yet lucid and easy, so perfectly achieved. I was gripped from the first page to the last." —Tessa Hadley, author of *The Past*

"An intense drama of classic themes—love, family, survival, and betrayal—told with passion and precision in Sahota's economical, lyrical prose. *China Room* is a brilliant novel. I won't forget any of these characters." —Adam Foulds, author of *The Quickening Maze*

"Such a thrilling combination of beauty and heartbreak. It's breathtaking." —Charlotte Mendelson, author of *When We Were Bad*

Praise for *China Room*

"An intimate page-turner with a deeper resonance as a tale of oppression, independence and resilience."
—*San Francisco Chronicle*

"Powerfully imagined." —*USA Today*

"Heart-wrenching." —*Entertainment Weekly*

"Sahota is a bold storyteller who seems to have learned as many tricks from TV as from Tolstoy, and has a jeweler's unillusioned eye for the goods. . . . Lovely phrases glitter . . . Sahota's ability to shine a phrase is not bought for the usual steep formalist price, at the expense of simplicity, intimate feeling, and solid representation. He's both camera and painter, in a literary world that often separates those novelistic tasks." —James Wood, *The New Yorker*

"[*China Room*] forges telling and skillful connections between the two very different eras, showing the ways that a place—a house, a room—can store up pieces of a remarkable past and release them, generations later, when someone comes looking."
—*The Wall Street Journal*

"A family saga both sweeping and granular . . . [that] examines agency, power, and human connection." —*Time*

"Gorgeously crafted . . . Powerful . . . A sweeping dual portrait."
—*Star-Tribune*

"[Sahota] is a restrained stylist whose details bloom in the imagination. . . . [There is] respite, even solace, to be found in [his] precise and exhilarating observation."
—Claire Messud, *Harper's Magazine*

"Intimate and startling." —*Electric Literature*

"A deeply captivating and necessary novel." —*Ploughshares*

"[*China Room*] illuminates the lives of those hidden away by history and the passage of time. . . . Sahota suggests that by unearthing their stories, we confront our individual and collective intergenerational pain." —*Washington Independent Review of Books*

"Beautifully realized . . . Sahota is a truly original novelist, his prose sparingly precise in its beauty, steeped in kindness and deep humanity." —*The Times Literary Supplement* (London)

"A multi-generational masterpiece." —*The Daily Mail* (London)

"Sahota feeds us big, difficult themes—segregation and freedom, revolution and empire . . . with poise, restraint and deep intelligence." —*The Times* (London)

"Engrossing . . . Intricate yet compact . . . The story's deceptively placid style renders its combustible elements all the more devastating. . . . [An] excellent novel." —*Literary Review* (London)

"[An] epic story about family secrets and the struggle to break free from the people and systems who try to hold others back." —*POPSUGAR*

"An examination of power and gender, *China Room* will make you reexamine a culture across time." —GoodMorningAmerica.com

"As beautiful as it is heart-shattering." —*Apartment Therapy*

"Compelling and devastating . . . Through short chapters and sparse, tightly wrought prose, Sahota's novel is both easy to read and difficult to put down. . . . Sahota cements his place in a vibrant literary canon alongside Salman Rushdie, Kamila Shamsie, Mohsin Hamid, Hari Kunzru, and others." —*BookPage*

PENGUIN BOOKS

CHINA ROOM

Sunjeev Sahota is the author of three novels: *China Room*, which was longlisted for the Booker Prize and was a finalist for the American Library Association's Carnegie Medal; *The Year of the Runaways*, which was shortlisted for the Booker Prize and the Dylan Thomas Prize, and was awarded a European Union Prize for Literature; and *Ours Are the Streets*. In 2013, he was named one of *Granta*'s twenty Best of Young British Novelists of the decade. He lives in Sheffield, England, with his family.

Penguin Reading Group Discussion Guide available online at penguinrandomhouse.com

SUNJEEV SAHOTA

CHINA ROOM

PENGUIN BOOKS

PENGUIN BOOKS
An imprint of Penguin Random House LLC
penguinrandomhouse.com

First published in Great Britain by Harvill Secker,
an imprint of Vintage, a division of Penguin Random House Ltd., 2021

First published in the United States of America by Viking,
an imprint of Penguin Random House LLC, 2021
Published in Penguin Books 2022

ISBN 9780593298220 (paperback)

THE LIBRARY OF CONGRESS HAS CATALOGED THE
HARDCOVER EDITION AS FOLLOWS:
Names: Sahota, Sunjeev, 1981– author.
Title: China Room / Sunjeev Sahota.
Description: [New York] : Viking, [2021]
Identifiers: LCCN 2021019350 (print) | LCCN 2021019351 (ebook) |
ISBN 9780593298145 (hardcover) | ISBN 9780593298213 (ebook)
Classification: LCC PR6119.A355 C49 2021 (print) |
LCC PR6119.A355 (ebook) | DDC 823/.92—dc23
LC record available at https://lccn.loc.gov/2021019350
LC ebook record available at https://lccn.loc.gov/2021019351

Printed in the United States of America
1 3 5 7 9 10 8 6 4 2

Set in Minion Pro

This is a work of fiction. Names, characters, places, and incidents either
are the product of the author's imagination or are used fictitiously, and any
resemblance to actual persons, living or dead, businesses, companies,
events or locales is entirely coincidental.

CHINA ROOM

1

Mehar is not so obedient a fifteen-year-old that she won't try to uncover which of the three brothers is her husband. Already, the morning after the wedding, and despite nervous, trembling hands, she combines varying amounts of lemon, garlic and spice in their side plates of sliced onions, and then attempts to detect the particular odour on the man who visits later that same night, invisible to her in the dark. It proves inconclusive, the strongest smell by far her fear, so she tries again after overhearing one of the trio complaining about the calluses on his hands. Her concentration is fierce when her husband's palm next strokes her naked arm, but then, too, she isn't certain. Maybe all male hands feel so rough, so clumsily eager and dry.

It is 1929, summer is erupting, and the brothers do not address her in one another's presence, indeed they barely speak to her at all, and she, it goes without saying, is expected to remain dutiful, veiled and silent, like the other new brides. Spying from her window, she sees only the brothers' likeness: close in age, they share the same narrow build, with unconvincing shoulders and grave eyes; serious faces that carry no slack, features that follow the same rules. The three are evenly bearded, the hair trimmed short and tight, and all day they wear loose turbans cut from the same saffron wrap. Most hours the brothers will be out working the fields, playing, drinking, while she weaves and cooks and shovels and milks, until those evenings when Mai, their mother, says to her, raising a tea-glass to grim lips:

'Not the china room tonight.'

This is the third time Mehar must finish washing the pewter pots at the courtyard water pump and, rather than join the women, take herself to the windowless chamber at the back of the farm. On the bed, she holds her knees close, seeing no point in lying down straight away. Five days married. Five nights since she'd first lain waiting in the pitch black, shuddering from arms to toes, hoping he wouldn't come to her and praying that there might be blood. The day before the wedding, Mehar's mother had folded a tiny blade into her daughter's hand. *Cut your thumb, to be sure.* Mehar hadn't done that, hadn't needed to, and Mai had been outside afterwards, waiting for the sheets. Her husband had said nothing to Mehar on that occasion, and little more on the next. Will he say more today, she wonders?

The tallow stick on its stony ledge has blown down to its crater and in the obliterating dazzle of the darkness she imagines she is underwater, in some submerged world of sea-goats and monsters. From across the court-yard she hears the distant protesting rasps of a charpoy and the scuffle of leather slippers being toed on. Her stomach does a small anticipatory flip, and she lies down as the door opens and he moves to sit at her side. She dares a sidelong glance at what must surely be his naked back, though it is impossible to make even a distinction between his hair and his cotton wrap, which she can hear him loosening. When she senses him unknotting the lan-got at his waist she averts her gaze to the black pool of the ceiling and waits.

'Undress,' he says, not unkindly, but with the contin-gent kindness of a husband who knows he will be obeyed. She tries to trap his voice inside her head, to parse its deep grain, its surprising hoarseness. Was he the one who'd called for more daal, who'd had her hurrying out to them earlier that day? She gathers the hem of her tunic up around her hips and unties her drawstring. She feels a rush of air against her calves as he slides off her salwar in a single swift motion, and then he bears down like something come to swallow her whole, until she can't even see the darkness on either side of him and fears that she really is inside his chest. He is neither rough nor gentle. A little frenetic perhaps, because all three brothers want a child, a child that must be a boy. Mehar's hands remain at her side, unmoving and cupped up. He smells strongly of grass and sweat, and of fenugreek and taro, the evening meal, but beyond that she can detect soap, and is glad that he had thought to wash before coming to her tonight. He grips her upper arm with one hand – calluses? Can she feel calluses? – then a final thrust, a stoppered exhalation, and he climbs off her, one leg at a time. His back to her again, she senses him return his penis into the pouch of his langot.

'You're learning the life here?'

'Everyone is very kind.'

He gives a wry little snort and she flicks her eyes towards the sound – nothing, she can see nothing. 'It's never been a kind house before,' he says, and shunts his feet back into the slippers.

2

The vessel is round, copper-bottomed, with a loop of a handle and a spout like a cobra rearing back for the strike. It's for the tea, this much they've been told, but how it is for the tea is not clear to them.

'It doesn't even lie flat,' Harbans says, confounded, holding the thing at arm's length as if it might curse her. 'And no hinges. Barely air to spread a fart in this room as it is.'

'The leaves go inside,' says Gurleen. She takes the contraption from Harbans and speaks as if all this would be obvious to anyone with a little breeding.

'So you've used one of these before?' asks Mehar, and Gurleen makes a frivolous face that tries to suggest she might have, once upon a time.

'You'll need the gauze,' says Harbans. She tips open one of the drawers and squints through the day-dark of the room. 'Lordy. The nice one for the three princes, yes?'

'Not so loud,' says Gurleen.

'A gauze over every cup?' asks Mehar, sounding doubtful.

Sisters together, they figure that the tea must be made in the usual way, in the brass pot and on the fire, and then strained into the copper vessel before being poured into cups, and all this they do, efficiently, sliding around each other in a space so narrow that when Mehar stands with her arms apart, her fingertips brush the walls. They live in the china room, which sits at a slight remove from the house and is named for the old willow-pattern plates that lean on a high stone shelf, a set of six that arrived with Mai years ago as part of her wedding dowry. Far beneath the shelf, at waist level, runs a concrete slab that the women use for preparing food, and under this is a modest mud-oven. The end of the room widens enough for a pair of charpoys to be laid perpendicular to each other and across these two string beds all three women are made to sleep.

'What a waste of time,' says Harbans, sieving the tea into the kettle. 'More things for me to wash.'

'It's how the English drink,' says Gurleen. 'Mai told me.' She's smiling at the thing, admiring the way its full bright sheen makes a reddish blur of her reflection. She tilts her face in profile. 'It looks so nice.'

'Mai speaks to you about these things?' asks Mehar, exchanging a droll look with Harbans.

'She's very nice to me. I think I remind her of her younger self.'

'Oh, you do?' says Mehar.

'We're both tall. Slim ...' A raised eyebrow towards Harbans. 'I imagine I'm married to the eldest.'

'Naturally,' says Mehar.

Gurleen was certainly those things, Mehar had to admit. Tall, slim – and beautiful. Though there was a tartness to her beauty, the tight dot of her lips, the hard diagonals of her cheekbones, that Mehar personally thought too much. The first time the three new brides had met and spoken, Mehar and Harbans had walked away readjusting their clothes, as if they'd just been browsed by Gurleen for signs of competition.

Harbans steps in. 'Go on then, mini-Mai, get this to them before big-Mai comes asking.'

The delight in Gurleen's face flees. 'Why me!'

'You said you know how,' Mehar reminds her, and she takes the kettle and presses it into Gurleen's hands, who resists until—

'Mehar!' calls Mai. 'Must we die of thirst?'

They freeze, and then Mehar mouths a scream and reaches for her veil.

The veil makes a red haze of everything, a sparkling opacity against which bodies move as dark shadows. It is pulled so far forward that it entirely conceals Mehar's face, and she must cast her eyes down to see anything at all. And what can she see? Her wrists, heavily bangled in red and white; the tea in her hands; and her painted feet, with the silver anklet bells announcing her journey over

7

the swept ground of the courtyard. Her hands shake with the fear that she's about to make a fool of herself, and, therefore, of the family. A tight slap awaits. The table inches into her vision and she stops, lingers, listens, though it's hard to hear over the clamour of her heart. It's so hot. She's hungry. How long ago was the midday meal? With her tongue she smears away the sweat from her top lip. Their talk quiets at her approach, as if in some strange deference.

'Please pour.'

His voice, she is sure of it. The same easy gruffness, the same clear brass. She thinks it came from her right. Without moving her head, she tries to peer through the top of her veil, where the chenille is thinner. It is impossible.

'Waiting for angels to shit?' snaps Mai.

Through the snake-spout, that is what they'd decided. Mehar takes a step closer and hears her anklet bells tinkle again. With one hand she holds the veil slightly away from her face and her field of vision is suddenly enlarged. The square brown table and four small glass cups, plain cups, set in a row. Mai, or Mai's feet, in their milk-green salwar, tapping the ground impatiently. Beside her the three sons, visible from the waist down only. One has a foot tucked under his thigh. Another sits with legs crossed. And the third: knees thrown apart, fingers drumming the oak frame of the charpoy. She is certain those must be his fingers, rough-looking. Callused hands. Callused! She bends and pours the tea, starting with Mai and working to the right, feeling relief when no challenge comes. His cup she leaves till last and as the tea flows she dares to raise her veil a little further, her face flushing as she takes in his handsome wrists, the way his white tunic sits over the attractive bump of his stomach, his open-necked collar …

'You can go,' says Mai, shrewd-eyed Mai, and at once Mehar drops her veil against her lips, her shoulders, so quickly that some of the material snags on her long lashes, and she turns and leaves.

3

On the nights when there is no tap on the shoulder from Mai, no instruction for anyone to go and wait in the rear chamber, Mehar gets in with Harbans in the china room. Gurleen takes the single, but she has pulled her pillow up so her head is right beside theirs. Tonight she fidgets, turning like a cheetah bothered by a fly.

'Sleep,' Mehar says. 'She'll have us up before dawn.'

'She'll have *me* up before dawn,' Harbans says, giving an immense yawn.

'God has built you to milk, Harbans: bucket arms, buffalo back,' Mehar tells her in a sombre voice that is perfectly Mai.

Harbans laughs and effortfully turns over, butting Gurleen, who sits up, knees raised and rocking in the dark. The bed squeaks.

'Sleep,' Mehar says again. 'Stop dwelling on it.'

'I can't,' Gurleen says. Then: 'I don't know why I'm here.'

'I wouldn't go thinking that way,' Harbans warns, in the direction of the wall.

'My baba promised me a rich city family. He said I'd be a memsahib.'

'Instead, here you are,' Mehar says, 'squeezed two to a bed with a pair of dream-free girls who feel like they've gone up in the world. Is that what you're saying?'

'I didn't mean it like that.'

'But that's how it sounds. We have to help each other now.'

'You milk mine and I'll milk yours,' adds Harbans.

'Exactly,' says Mehar. 'You're not still brooding about the kettle, are you?'

The embarrassment makes Gurleen's eyes sting all over again.

They'd called for more tea and she had blocked Mehar at the door and announced that she'd do it. She could impress her husband too, whichever of the three he might be. She pulled her veil low and sashayed over and poured with real flourish, the tea arcing gracefully and each cup filled precisely, identically. Then one of the brothers spoke:

'Not for me. It can go back in.' A hand crept into her circle of vision, nudging the cup towards the middle of the table.

She stood there holding the kettle. Go back in? But how? This was not something she and her new sisters had discussed. She felt the walls of her throat dry out. In her mind's eye she could see them all staring at her, this woman who was disobeying a man of the family, embarrassing her husband, so she picked up the glass and tried to pour the tea back in via the spout. She was spilling it everywhere and half in tears when Mai said – barked, to Gurleen's ear – to just take the glass to the kitchen, where Mehar and Harbans were biting their laughter into closed fists.

'We shouldn't have laughed,' Mehar now admits. 'I'm sorry.'

'Why didn't I just lift the lid?'

'You panicked.'

'They'll think I'm stupid.'

'Let them think what they want.'

'I won't let them think me an imbecile.'

'How posh she talks!' says Harbans.

Gurleen sighs and lifts her face to the ceiling. Closes her eyes. 'I think I need some air.'

'Just lie back down,' says Mehar, beginning to tire of Gurleen's self-pity. 'Here. Hold my hand.'

Then, from Harbans: 'That's my foot.'

Laughter. It makes Mehar feel bold. She shifts, turns over, the rough weaves creaking. 'So does yours talk to you? Properly?'

'A little bit,' says Gurleen, cautiously. 'He swears a lot. Not at me. Just to himself. Does yours?'

'Do you know which one yours is?'

'Of course not.'

12

'You know, I might just ask Mai,' Mehar says, if only to provoke Gurleen, who near chokes and asks her if she's gone mad.

'Mine called me a big strong girl,' Harbans says. 'During. He slapped my behind and called me a big strong girl.'

All three chuckle, though real tears come to Harbans' eyes, which she knuckles away. Mehar reaches out to touch her shoulder.

'Mine doesn't say much,' says Mehar, and remembers him calling this an unkind house. She imagines what the place might have been like before, when it was only Mai and her three sons, and it chills her to realise that she can't hear any laughter. Her eyes move to the closed window, the only one in this room of unpainted stone. It has no glass and its black lacquered slats must be turned individually, by hand. Did Mai also stand there, looking out, when she was young and newly married?

'You two have a lot to learn,' says Gurleen, seizing a chance to reassert some dominance. She gets herself comfortable on the charpoy again, her head on the pillow. 'Where's my shawl? I can hear a mosquito.'

'Here, sisters,' says Mehar, and they each take a corner of the shawl and billow it out so it floats down and over their faces.

4

It is their second Sunday married and an hour before the sun drops, Mehar, Gurleen and Harbans slip into some old cottons and heave the giant sloshing vat into the courtyard and on to the groundsheet. At this hour the air is lushly warm rather than oppressive and the courtyard is free of the brothers. They think their men go to the bazaar on these nights, though that is another thing they have never been told. Perhaps they play cards, Mehar suggests, as if she knows what that is. All three hitch up their salwars and twine some old jute around their legs, so they're naked from the knees down. 'The leaves have come up,' Gurleen says, feeling for a way out of the chore, a rare one she finds even more tedious than rubbing clean the spinach. But Harbans is having none of it and points out that there is still plenty of ink left in them. They hold hands, forming a triad, and one by one step inside the metal vat, the indigo plants sliding around the soles of their feet. The water, as if answering a question, rises up to their calves and their feet begin their work, up-down-up-down, a surging spilling tempest, the colour wrenched out and out. They do not speak, it is enough to try to keep their balance, and slowly the pool starts to darken, their clothes and skin too, indigo staining legs and hips and face, but they stay in harmony, up-down-up-down, minutes upon minutes, so that by the time the sun has disappeared and the moon is the whole light, they let go of one another's hands and double over, gasping.

'One more week,' Harbans says, as they haul the vat back to its spot against the wall.

'Oh, go crack an egg! Surely we're done now!' Gurleen complains.

Mehar says nothing, picks up the crumbling soap at the pump and starts on the blue bands striping her feet. It's up to Mai, in any case. She will decide when the time is right to colour their blooded wedding sheets and hang them out to dry.

5

'Mehar! The fire needs kindling!'

'Yes, Mai!' Mehar sighs, placing down the bucket of milk and turning indoors, her thoughts wheeling.

She is shovelling out the old ashes when Mai enters and kicks the flour barrel to see how much the girls are using for themselves.

'You three guzzle more than the men,' Mai says. 'Halve it next time.'

'As you wish. But we only eat—'

'Are any of you seeded yet?' Mai asks, in a grotesque swerve.

'No, Mai.' Be strong, she reminds herself. Her hands slow in their work. 'I wondered if sister Gurleen should have her child first. She's the eldest.'

'The fool doesn't know which way round a kettle goes.'

Mehar takes a breath, in through her nose, out from her mouth. 'Is she also married to the eldest?'

When she looks up, Mai is gazing at her silently, a look of horrible amusement on her face.

'We don't need to know,' Mehar says in a rush, wishing she'd never asked.

'Are you certain I send the same son to you each time?' Mai's expression gives in to a huge laugh: 'The look on you!' She strokes Mehar's hair, a touch that Mehar hates, that feels far from maternal. 'I'm only playing. But you're right. You don't need to know.' Her face changes, the smile faltering. 'Be thankful you've no father-in-law to paw and prowl over your body every night.' She pats Mehar's head in a leave-taking gesture. 'Ashes. Carry on,' and Mehar does, industriously, desperate to finish up and wash herself for an hour or more. If this is how asking the question makes her feel, she'll never ask again. She'll just do the work. And she does, they do:

Breaking up blocks of jaggery. Picking cotton. Picking guavas. Collecting dung. Shovelling ashes. Cutting Mai's corns. Milking. Cooking. Preparing for the cooking. Dyeing salwars. Ironing dhotis. Sweeping the yard. Watering the yard. Draining the yard. Polishing the plates. Going to market. Going to temple. Going to pray for sons and for the long life of their husbands. Scrubbing the stone bath clean of moss. Sewing buttons. Boiling tea. Midwifing calves. Removing buffalo shit. Going for a shit amongst the high wheat (in pairs). Bathing before dawn. Eating last of all. In their room by dusk. Slats turned, window shut, moon out, veils off. Yet more darkness.

6

'You're used to this life now.'

He strokes Mehar's anklebone with his thumb, back and forth, back and forth. It tickles and she wants to move her foot but knows she mustn't. She can see nothing of him. When he stepped across the room and lifted his knee on to the bed, he moved through blackness. When he was on top of her she, like any respectable wife, averted her head. Still he strokes her anklebone. It's as if he wants to say something. Or perhaps she's the one who should be doing the saying? No. No. *You'll know when to open your mouth.*

'We went to see the priests.'

Ah. Children.

'Pearls. I need to buy pearls. If you keep them under the bed you will swell. Glow. A boy.'

'Yes,' she says, after a moment.

She thinks she hears him nod or sigh and before he departs he closes his hand around her entire ankle and presses.

Alone, Mehar exhales with relief, rising in the same breath, and reties her hair into the nape of her neck. Children, she thinks, and sits very still in the dark to discover what she really feels about the prospect. On the one hand, the sooner sons arrive, the sooner her presence in the house is secure. Not everyone is as forgiving as her father, willing to overlook a wife who can't birth males, refusing to switch her for another who can. But, then again, once her child comes her few moments of peace will be gone. At least now, when Mai's out, she and Harbans can steal across the yard for a nap in the shade. What hope for that when her son is latched to her breast? Mehar's hand goes to her neck, protectively, as if only now appreciating the luxury of being alone with herself. Another minute passes, two, until she knows she must go, and she drapes her chunni over her head, ready to yank down the veil should she need to. She opens the door and the cool marble meets her feet – *her* feet – as she steps outside. She feels suddenly alive, enough to levitate into the night, and it is an immense effort to remain grounded, here in this horseshoe of a yard with the three doors all opposite. Which did he enter, if any? Mehar descends the two steps that take her beyond the overhang of the veranda and on to the outer yard, where she knows to duck for the bats flying overhead and to avoid the deep divot to her right, walking a path between the washing line and the charpoys piled against the wall. At the unmarbled entrance to the china room she places her fingernails in the one spot where the door can be prised open and not make a sound. She does all this without pause or misstep because in a purely practical sense (she gets in beside Harbans) her husband is right: she is already used to this life, to this small world of hers, which is, she is now saddened to recall, just what Monty said would happen.

7

Around ten years earlier – for who can be sure? – Mehar spent most afternoons playing pittu in the hot cobbled lanes around her house. You had to stack seven stones in a tall pile before everyone on your team was struck by the opposition's hard leather ball. Mehar, aged five, loved the game and was so quick at it. She was always first to be picked after the boys and today she'd also been the last of her team to be got out, but not before she'd picked off three from the other side, more than any other player – these were the thoughts crowding her head as she came rushing home only to be brought up short by the sight of two guests she did not recognise. They were not her aunts or uncles, nor were they anyone she knew from the village. Mehar, who was not called Mehar then, came slowly, watchfully, down the uncovered passageway, in and out of shadow. They hadn't yet noticed her. The guests seemed friendly, she had to admit, sitting in the shaded half of the small square courtyard. She could see empty glasses of tea on the table along with a fussy plate of mangoes, sliced lengthways and sprinkled with some green herb. There was also a round steel tea-bowl covered with a lemon-pale cloth.

'Ah, here she is!' said her baba, with a smile as wide as a river, because too long in the company of adults was always difficult for him. His name was Arvind and though he had the spirit of a child, he seemed to be trying very hard to look serious today. He was wearing English trousers instead of his usual dhoti, and his turban seemed far too neat, all of which made Mehar nervous. 'Come here,' he said, and Mehar obliged, sitting beside her baba on the charpoy, her head snug against his armpit. She looked up into the hot blue sky and momentarily wondered what might be on the other side of the sun, but it was too white and it hurt. Her gaze fell back down, to her ordinary courtyard and these four oddly smiling adults.

'Lovely features,' said the female guest, whose smile seemed more tepid than her husband's, her eyes more sly.

'Mustard oil works wonders, when we can get it, but who can these days?' said Mehar's mother apologetically.

Simran was, even in the natural course of things, a very apologetic woman, a state that had only deepened following her failure to conceive another child. Her hands were in her lap and her painted – why were they painted? – thumbnails fidgeted against each other. Her daughter's arrival seemed to have increased her anxiety and her ma,

Mehar noticed, was not at all looking towards the other woman, who, for some reason, was very blatantly appraising Mehar.

'I think she has a nice face,' Simran ventured, 'and, god willing, I'm sure she'll grow into her forehead. Rest assured, I apply downward pressure on it most mornings,' she finished, smiling, not smiling, smiling again.

'Uff, her forehead's fine,' Arvind said. He turned to the male guest. 'If they're not washing their faces in cream, they're pinching pegs on to their noses, and if not that then kneading the hell out of their foreheads. You're lucky you've only sons. You must save a fortune in milk.'

The man laughed, a full bright overcooked laugh that made his wife wince. 'What we save in milk we lose in flour. The rotis can't come fast enough, isn't that right?'

His wife, who was, of course, Mai, didn't answer. She made a quarter turn of her knees towards Simran, tacitly suggesting that there'd been enough jibber-jabber and it was time to get down to business. 'She's adequate,' she said, with the lavish rudeness a woman rich in sons finds easy to dispense. 'In any case, an agreement was made. Shall we move on?'

Mehar's mother nodded, with difficulty, and when tears sprang to her eyes, Mehar noticed her baba raise his hand in a caring, calming gesture. Was her ma leaving? Was Baba not going to do something?

The woman unknotted her cloth bag smartly, with her long fingers and longer palms, and lifted out a heavy-looking scarlet chunni, all sequined lozenges and gold tasselled trim.

Mehar reached across and touched the tassels, which felt creepily ticklish. The man laughed, too loudly. His eyes were very red.

'She likes it … It's for you, you know.'

Mehar wanted to protest, to say that he was mistaken, that she found it revolting and didn't want it at all, but she had a feeling she'd been caught in something too big and would be better off standing aside while the situation passed by. She returned to her baba, who picked her up by her armpits and planted her in the middle of the group. Mehar made to return to her spot but her baba's 'Nup!' stayed her. The woman billowed out the scarlet chunni behind Mehar, then set it across her head and down her sides. She held her palm out towards her husband, who placed into it a crisp tan two-and-a-half-rupee note, which she touched to Mehar's forehead before passing it to Simran. Simran then retrieved from her wedding cupboard in the inner room a glass pot of salt and handed it to her in exchange.

'There was no need,' the woman said, pocketing it all the same. 'It's got so expensive nowadays.'

'Which of your sons have you decided upon for her?' Arvind asked.

The woman spoke before her husband could answer. 'Where's the rush? Details can be agreed later. For now …' And she pulled the large brocaded chunni down over Mehar's eyes, her mouth, all the way to her stomach, and Mehar realised with a sudden thick panic in her chest that it was her they had come to wrap up and take away.

'Her new name is Mehar Kaur. And may she bring mercy with her.'

That evening, with the awful guests gone and, moreover, gone without her, Mehar made a start on her father's shirt. For some weeks now, Simran had been building up Mehar's repertoire of household chores, fortifying her daughter with those skills that would prove most useful in her new life. Weaving baskets, separating lentils, catching mice, and, as now, ironing. Mehar spat into the oven and the coals hissed theatrically. Gingerly, she leaned in with a long-handled spoon and extracted all three pieces from the fire, dropped them into a flat-bottomed brass jar, and gripping the pot under its thick lip, ran to the room where she'd laid the shirt out on a muslin blanket. As she pressed the hot bottom of the jar across the rough cotton, in and out of the creases, her tongue between her teeth, the repetition of the act sent her mind back to the guests, to the stern woman with the thin face and skinned-back hair. Not nice people. And not allowed back, she told herself, even as she touched her forehead experimentally. What was wrong with her forehead?

She snapped out of it when Monty's silhouette appeared across the red glaze of the window. He was Mehar's cousin and had been living with them for several months, sent by his mother (Simran's sister, who'd birthed two sons) to help on the land until such time as Simran delivered a boy of her own. It was a situation the eight-year-old Monty still resented and Mehar ignored him as he entered the room and searched under the charpoy and behind the incense burners lined unevenly upon the shelves. His hair was clipped short, his sleeves sliced off at the shoulder, and his movements were quick and abrupt, as if living here made him flinch.

'Have you seen my spittoon?' he asked.

Mehar smacked her tongue against the roof of her mouth – no.

'Hell.' He stepped towards her. 'Do mine next?'

'Where is it?'

He paused. 'Your front teeth overlap. Did you know that?'

Her forehead *and* her front teeth. With great forbearance, Mehar smiled, carried on with her work, but Monty continued, his grievance against this family fuelling him on.

'Those people here earlier. You know you're marrying their son?'

'I'm not,' Mehar said calmly, used to Monty's nastiness. 'They've gone, anyway.'

He raised one foot on to the charpoy, deliberately mussing her ironing, and ran his hand down his shin. Mehar pulled the muslin blanket taut again.

'You'll be going to live with them soon. They've even changed your name.'

'That's silly,' Mehar said, though it disturbed her that Monty seemed to be repeating something her baba had mentioned a few hours ago, after they'd gone. Back then, she hadn't been really listening, too busy with the elation of the guests departing alone.

26

'Maybe their son chose your new name.'

'Which son?'

'The one you're going to marry and live with.'

And now Mehar was starting to panic again, the same wildness she'd felt when they'd pulled the scarlet chunni down over her face.

'I think your grandfather and their grandfather were friends. They'd shaken hands on it or something.'

He really did sound like he knew a lot, Monty did. 'Shut up,' Mehar said, feeling suddenly hot and tearful and overwhelmed. 'Or I'll burn you.'

'You'll burn that shirt first,' Monty warned, and Mehar removed the jar to the steel plate. 'Oh, God,' he continued, 'I hope your mother gives you a brother soon or I bet I'll end up carrying you into the temple. What's taking them so long?'

She didn't want anyone carrying her in anywhere, ever. She looked down at the shirt, fighting tears, and then, with the same calm stoicism she often overheard her mother praising, looked up into Monty's face. 'When will I have to go? Can I see Diwali first?'

'In about ten years,' Monty said, authoritatively, and Mehar's eyes widened in euphoria and a small laugh burst out of her mouth, because ten years were unimaginable: twice as long as she'd already been on this earth, yes, she knew that, and yet strangely incalculable in all the ways that mattered. Each year seemed to contain so many more, the seasons stretching on and on, so much so that Monty might as well have said 'never', and thoughts

of marriage slipped away, away and down the drains outside their house, only resurfacing when Mehar was eleven
and Monty came running up the stairs and on to the
roof, his slippers quick against the concrete.

'Your mother-in-law's here!' he gasped.

Mehar had been playing pat-a-cake with one of the
neighbours' toddlers, both of their faces painted in the
black and red of Kali, for Dussehra would be upon
them in a few days. 'Who? Here now?' she said and he
lunged for her arm and pulled her towards the stairs.
'But my face!'

'She asked to see you straight away. Ma sent me.'
Monty had been with the family for so long now that he
had taken to calling Mehar's mother Ma, and Simran's
sister, the woman who birthed him and whom he saw
perhaps once a year, he addressed as Massi, as like-a-
mother. At the bottom of the stairs they slowed and
Monty, still with his hand around Mehar's wrist, led her
to the window at the rear of the yard and peered into
the house. Dust idled in shafts of sunlight. On a brown,
bruised-looking settee sat Mai, straight-backed, nib-
bling decorously at a sweetmeat while Ma violently
fanned her.

'Has someone died?' Monty asked. 'She's in white.'

Mehar made a face, as if to say, how would she know?

'Go and wash that rubbish off,' Monty hissed, and
Mehar took a careful step back and was inching towards
the water pump when someone spoke from inside.

'Mehar, come in here at once.'

Mehar looked to Monty, alarm in her eyes as she pointed to her blackened face, to the devil's red tongue painted down her chin.

'She can't bear to come to you empty-handed, dearest aunty,' Monty said. 'Please allow her to arrive at your feet with an offering of lemon-water.'

'I've had water. What I don't have is time to wait. In here now.'

Mehar shook her head and her hands, and took another step back.

'Please don't embarrass her by forcing her into your orbit with nothing to give,' Monty replied, his fist at his mouth.

'Mehar Kaur' – this was Ma – 'your mother has come to see you. Inside, this second.'

Mehar's shoulders fell, defeated, and she took a moment to prepare her apology before stepping across the yard. As she passed Monty, he hastily uncoiled the grubby, white wrap from his hair, shook it out with a single snap of the material and draped it over her head and down her face.

'It's see-through,' Mehar whispered.

'Not enough to worry about. Keep looking at the floor,' he murmured, as he opened the wooden door and followed her in.

Mehar touched Mai's toes, then took a seat opposite her, beside Simran.

'There are no unfamiliar men here,' Mai said.

'She's grieving,' Monty said.

'Who for?' Mai asked.

'For whoever has passed,' he said, gesturing at her own white clothes.

'You do not know who you are grieving for?'

Mai's tone left no doubt that she wanted only Mehar to speak, and so, behind the makeshift veil, she mouthed a silent prayer and took a chance: 'I had a vision that my father was not well and when I saw that today you made that long journey alone, I felt God tell me to enter into a period of mourning.'

There was a sudden swelling stillness. For a daughter-in-law even to think of her father-in-law's death, let alone voice it aloud, was unforgivably insolent. The waiting silence ballooned and was punctured by the sound of humming; they all turned to watch as the neighbour's child padded down the stairs, crossed the yard and disappeared into the passageway.

'He died nearly a month ago,' Mai said. 'His heart gave way.'

Simran laid down the fan, about to summon up the required amount of tears, but Mai warded them off with a raised hand.

'What's done is done. He served us well.' She ploughed on with a sigh. 'I've brought your official mourning clothes.' From her cloth bag, she took a brown parcel secured with red-and-white twine and passed it to Simran to hand across to Mehar.

'I will wear them for a full year,' Mehar said seriously. 'I will honour my father's life.'

'A week will do. Winter's coming.' Mai stood. 'Would you accompany me to the door, Mehar.' It was not a question.

They went down the passageway together, Mehar half a step behind Mai because the path was too narrow. The light never fully penetrated this part of the house, this alley linking home-yard to village lane, lending it all a secretive, confidential air.

'What other visions have you had?'

'This was my first.'

Mai made a noise of assent. 'Have you started bleeding yet?'

'Yes,' Mehar replied, feeling herself redden.

'Perhaps that did it.'

They'd reached the threshold of the passageway and Mehar waited for Mai to step into the lane, turn round and allow Mehar to touch her feet in farewell. She wanted her gone so she could rush back inside and laugh about it all with Monty. Mai, however, moved closer to Mehar and pushed her against the cold stones of the wall. She felt Mehar's breasts, coarsely, squeezing them hard through the tunic, using all her fingers and the heel of her palm. Though it hurt and her mouth dropped open, Mehar said not a word, her arms limp at her side.

'Get some unstitched cloth and wrap it round and round. Tight as your cunt. They must be kept small. We're not a family of obscenities.'

Mehar nodded.

'You are a pretty little thing.' Mai smiled. 'And the next time I ask you to come to me you'll come straight away, won't you?'

Mehar nodded again, and perhaps it was the gulp disappearing into Mehar's throat that widened the smile on Mai's lips.

'Well done.' She kissed Mehar's forehead through the material, told her to enjoy Dussehra, and strode out into the sunny lane, not permitting Mehar to ask for a farewell blessing.

Mehar walked back down the passageway, feeling disturbed and dislocated by the encounter, but stepping into the light of the courtyard had a galvanising effect, wrenching her back into the known world. She ran into the room, where Monty was bent double and laughing so hard that tears were visible.

'Your brother's gone chukpatty crazy,' her mother said, only to let out a loud yelping gasp of her own when a grinning Mehar tore away her veil.

They recounted that afternoon many times over the following months, always with embellishments from Monty. 'The witch even went to lift the veil, but quick as lightning I interjected with a plate of sweetmeats,' he said to Mehar's father. 'Uncle, you should have seen her face as I kept stopping her from getting a look at our Mehar!' But as months produced years, it was spoken of less and less, reprised for one last time a few weeks before the wedding. Mai was set to pay them a final visit and had sent word, via a travelling sadhu, that on this occasion she'd be arriving with one of her sons.

'Kali Mata would scare him off. Still got the guts?' Monty said, as Mehar mixed a little more ghee into the soot. She took a small flint from the top of the mirror and lined her eyes with kajal. It was just the two of them in this new room that her father had built on to the roof, and as he joined her on the broad green cushion of the stool, Monty, seventeen years old and searching for a bride of his own, looked every inch the disapproving older brother.

'I'll tell you something for free. I'll never ever ask my wife to make-up herself. I'll forbid it.'

Mehar smiled through her nerves and patted his hand, which had been resting on her shoulder this whole time. She loved him, uncomplicatedly. When she'd got him alone one evening a few moons after Mai had manhandled her, Mehar had asked him what her cunt was and Monty had held her close and told her not to worry about things like that, which had only confused her further, more so because she could feel against her own chest the small sobs coming from his.

'I think they're here,' Mehar said, standing, licking her finger and running it along her eyebrows. Nerves or not, there was no point in waiting. You couldn't outrun your fate.

'Ants in your pants?' Monty said. He tugged her back down as he stood up, as if a pulley operated them both. 'We'll call you when we're ready.'

An hour passed and still Mehar was waiting in the rooftop room. She could hear their voices, muffled, and the rattling of crockery as teas and sweetmeats were passed round. She dared not sneak outside and glance over the wall, knowing the squeal of the doors would give her away, especially now winter had come and the black grease was impossible to get hold of. Instead, she brought out the jamawar shawl from under the charpoy and freed it of its paper wrapping. It was a beautiful thing, all burnt umbers and handwoven browns, stitched and decorated with care and delicacy to reveal some fresh pattern every time Mehar looked at it. The intricate red border ('French embroidery,' the seller had said, bafflingly) felt like a caress against her cheek. Mehar loved the texture of it in her hands, and the feeling of owning something so ravishing. She was certain her mother-in-law would love it too, that it would only elevate Mehar's standing in her new family, because the shawl was the most captivating element of Mehar's trousseau, and, along with new furniture, two bulls and five burlaps of grain, would form part of Mehar's procession at the end of the wedding. She kissed the shawl, rewrapped and returned it under the charpoy, and then, not entirely accidentally, stood to find that she was once more assessing herself in the long wardrobe mirror. Her turquoise tunic with gold trim and matching salwar had been a congratulatory gift from her maternal grandmother, who'd made the three-day journey to her daughter's house six months ago. On Mehar's feet were gold satin slippers, the seams scratching against the arch of each foot. Her hair, washed, oiled, combed, hung in a single plait down her back. She tried to peer at herself from the corner of her eye, to catch herself unaware, as if that might enable a more candid assessment: the pale mouth, the wheatish complexion, the large – some said too large – eyes. Would I think I was beautiful?

'Come on.'

She turned round, unstartled despite not hearing Monty come in, nodded once and reached for her chunni, wearing it like a veil.

Monty steered her down the stairs, whispering inanities: 'So big, I'm not sure if he's man or elephant,' and, 'Did they tell you about his missing teeth?'

She wasn't sure if he was trying to comfort her or distract himself from his own grief. In any case, she played along and elbowed his ribs, hissing: 'You'll make me trip.'

In the courtyard, Mehar steeled herself, pressed her lips together and tried to remember that she had nothing to worry about. She harboured a lingering fear of his mother, true, but Mai had approved her. They wouldn't – surely couldn't – go back on it all now, at this late stage, even if he thought her as ugly as a wild pig. She touched her forehead, as though pressing it back into place, a tic whose origin she could no longer recall. Then the door was opened and she walked inside, her eyes cast down. All she could see was floor, and the floor's odd faded chalk lines that she didn't think she'd ever noticed before. Monty's hand at her back guided her to a seat and, lowering herself with infinite care, she recognised her mother's feet to her right and, on her left, her father's sandals, his squared-off toenails. The table was laid in front of her. Empty cups, plates still piled high with sweetmeats, miniature bowls of half-eaten faluda.

They were talking politics and had been for some while because this marriage was taking place at a time of horrific and continuing falls in crop prices. The English mills had ceased buying, the viceroys had simultaneously raised rents, and local farmers were being forced to sell (to the canny British, no less) what gold they still had so that they might keep hold of their land. All things that, up and down the country, were sparking anti-British marches and freedom movements.

'It'll end in riots if they're not careful.'

Mehar listened hard over the sound of her heart's hammering. That must be him. He sounded strong and forceful, tall and handsome. The thrills of projection!

He continued: 'Everywhere you go, there are agitators.'

'Anyone can agitate. It takes real guts to take the fight to them,' said Monty.

'I'm sure you've guts for all of us,' Mai's son replied, eliciting a little laughter from the room.

They continued like this, as if Mehar hadn't even joined them, until Simran (as she must) asked if she might make another pan of tea and Mai (as she must) declined, saying time was moving on and they'd have to leave soon if they wanted to miss the Mussulmans, today being their godforsaken Friday. That seemed to be the sign Simran had been waiting for, and Mehar felt her mother's arm come around her back and saw her rouged fingertips pinching the hem of the veil. She unveiled Mehar as if she were raising a curtain, and throughout the ordeal Mehar held her breath, quivering with nerves, listening for gasps of horror, praying that there wouldn't be any. Finally, Simran folded the veil across Mehar's head and they all sat in silence while Mehar, still trembling, continued to fix her gaze to the ground. She knew she didn't possess the audacity to look up into his face. From Monty, Mehar would later learn that at this point Mai and her son exchanged a confirmatory look, before the woman said, 'I spoke to our priest and the stars look auspicious next month, preferably on the seventeenth day.'

'We'd be delighted to welcome you and your son on whichever day best suits you,' Arvind said, sounding distinctly relieved.

'I'll confirm by telegram,' Mai said. 'My other sons are marrying too.' She spoke with measured boastfulness. 'We came straight from the other girls' homes, hence our late arrival. Three weddings, one ceremony. I'll send word once we've finalised the date.'

'As you wish,' said Arvind, though his voice betrayed a slight confusion.

'But is it you my sister will be marrying?' asked Monty, a question that almost earned him a slap once the guests had departed and Simran stormed that he had no right being so impertinent.

The old witch (Monty later said) had been about to speak, when the son cut in: 'That decision will be made in consultation with my younger brothers. But you need not worry. I promise you that your sister will be marrying one of us,' he finished, to more nervous laughter from Mehar's parents.

Such arrangements weren't new – far from it – but Monty was incensed and, later, during his outburst with Simran, said that this was the twentieth century, for pity's sake. Mehar had the right to know who she'd be marrying.

'She has the right to be married into a good family and these are good Kala Sanghian people. The specific man doesn't matter. A real brother would see that,' Simran added, in a hurtful swipe uncharacteristic of her, which only made the wound slice deeper.

As they entered the new month and the seventeenth drew closer, preparations for the day – are there enough blankets if the guests are cold? Have the chamars been bribed to steer clear of the temple? – overwhelmed any thoughts of who precisely Mehar would be following around the holy book. Mehar, too, tried not to worry. Her mother was right: what difference would it make? It was not as if she'd be able to reject the boy, or say, *No, thank you, I'll take the other one instead*, as though she were choosing eggs in the market.

On the wedding day itself no one in the family knew for sure who she'd ended up with. Mehar was shrouded from head to foot in her heavy red gown and gold drapes, her hands and even her feet wrapped in chenille, the material folded back and bound with gold threads around her ankles and wrists. She couldn't walk, talk or hear, and neither was she expected to, so Monty carried her across his arms, from the cart, up the steps, through the half-full temple and seated her beside the man waiting near the front of the hall. The groom wore his sehra, his curtain of white marigolds braided with crimson blooms, clipped to his turban and hanging down over his face. Monty tried to see if it was the same man who'd come to the house, and perhaps he managed to. Who knows? Even had he succeeded, there was no way of delivering news to Mehar. Having carried her to the groom, he found no other opportunity to speak to her that day: once the ceremony was over she followed her husband into the cart, the driver kicked the horses into action and Monty, determined not to cry, never saw his sister again.

✳✳✳

In July 2019 my father underwent surgery to have his entire left knee replaced. After four days in hospital he was discharged with a blister pack of pain relief, some blood thinner, a pamphlet promoting ten lots of exercises, and a pair of crutches. He and Mum were going to need daily help on all sorts of fronts, so my wife and three kids drove down to my in-laws for the summer while I returned to the house and shop where I grew up, moving back into my old bedroom, behind a door that still read S—'s. Some of my duties rendered me to my teenaged self: Mum calling me down to unload a delivery, or to drive over to the cash-and-carry in the van, or trudge out with the newspapers because the paperboy was hungover from the night before. When it came to Dad, it was all new. I held his hand while he completed circuits of the dining table. I bore his weight up and down the stairs. I removed his

40

compression socks and moisturised his massively swollen, woody and unflexing leg. I helped him dress. I also had to show people round, because the knee surgery had finally forced Dad, however recalcitrantly, and after thirty-one years, into putting the place up for sale. So there I was, hurrying prospective buyers past Dad lying on the sofa, who far from acknowledging their bright hellos, pointed his crutch after them like some sniper. He was going to miss the place desperately, and something like sweet melancholy filled those sunny afternoons when people came to tramp in and out of the rooms.

By the second week, the three of us seemed to have found our groove, a routine. I came to recognise once again the 6 a.m. sounds of the milk-and-bread man, sounds that had me crushing toast into my mouth and heading out to agree our order. Twenty years on, I was again totting up the takings, allowing for the Lottery, the Instants, the Paypoint cash, mindful that a float needed to be left in the till. I adjusted my meal plans once Mum reminded me (how could I have forgotten?) that Dad liked raita only with his evening meal, not his afternoon one. I didn't have much spare time, but between cooking and showing people round, fetching Dad his Codeine and administering the Tinzaparin, between helping him through his exercises and helping Mum with the shop, I tried to read. I'd brought a pile of books with me: *The Little Virtues*; *Under the Volcano*; a biography of Leonora Carrington; Les Murray's *Waiting for the Past*. Though I realised it only later, the books were all by or about people who had already taken their leave. Not that I read any of them: I was too distracted, my mind too tense. I couldn't give my attention to comprehending someone else's world when I was, for the first time in two decades – and for the final time, too – living in the place that had once unravelled my own. Instead, I'd sit at the dining table in the late evenings, with overlarge images of Sikh gurus on the wall behind me and family photographs on the wall ahead.

There was one photo that I'd focus on, a small picture in a dark-wood frame. It was of my great-grandmother, an old white-haired woman who'd travelled all the way to England just so that she might hold me, her new-born great-grandson. She's looking down and smiling, unused to a camera's eye, her chunni sliding off her head. I am screaming. The photo hung there quietly as I sat at the table, opened up my laptop and started to write. I realised then that by leaving all those books unread I'd been clearing the ground the better to see what was in front of me, which was the past. All sorts of pasts, in fact, including one that found me rehabilitating on a farm in India, in 1999, the summer after I turned eighteen.

'You should have called from the station,' my uncle said, as he struggled with my case and, in the end, abandoned it halfway up the stairs with a little pat on its head. We were inside his tall house in the village of Kala Sanghian. 'I'd have come to get you.'

'You should have called from England,' my aunt said. 'Ambushing us like this. It shows no respect. None at all.'

'Oh, we knew you were coming.'

'Not which day we bloody didn't.'

'Yes,' my uncle conceded, wincing, smiling with embarrassment. 'But he's here now.'

Aunt Kuku stared at me sceptically. Her wide heavy face drooped forward at the neck, as if she'd been gently drugged, but her eyes were alert. Surely she was contrasting the healthy, plump-cheeked boy of four years ago with the young man in front of her now: too skinny, too pinched, too drawn. I felt myself squirming under her gaze, looking left and right in an effort to shrug it off, and then I remembered the duty-free in my rucksack and presented my uncle the bottle of Glenfiddich. He turned it round in his hand, admiringly, and placed it on the table between us.

'You drink?' Kuku asked.

'Sometimes,' I said.

'A man now, isn't he,' Jai said approvingly. He was short, with a big, teddy-bear belly and a naked, youthful face clear of any wrinkles. His inch-high pelt of glossy hair was, unlike his wife's, entirely untroubled by grey. A friendly enough man, but no match for her, so everyone said. There was a rumour she'd slapped him once, in the first month of their marriage, for raising his voice to her. Been silent ever since, the gossips tittered.

'One last holiday before university, yes? Is that what this is?'

'Thanks for letting me stay.'

'Silliness,' Jai said. 'But the heat will only get worse, you know.'

I felt a sudden, violent clenching in my stomach and I pulled my lips into my mouth and trapped them between my teeth, hard. The pain backed off, as quickly as it had pounced, but it left its mark, its warning, as if someone had smiled at me from the wings, all threat. I tried to tune back into whatever my uncle was saying, but he was looking at me expectantly, then with confusion, a single crease folding his brow.

'So will you?'

'Sorry?'

'What's the matter with you?' Kuku said.

'Turn the geyser clockwise when having a cold shower?' Jai said.

'Shall we have that drink now?' I said, motioning for the bottle.

'Son, it's not even nine yet,' he replied, but I was already on my feet and carrying the bottle to the fridge. When I opened the door, the fridge's humming got louder, a drilling in my ear. I took out the jug of water and grabbed two tumblers from a high shelf dressed in doilies. They were both looking at me (he agape, she calm) as I returned with the whiskies and passed him his. I raised my glass in an unspecified toast and downed about half.

I'd got steadily through three-quarters of the bottle when Jai, without a word, removed the whisky from the table and took it downstairs. I heard a lock turning. When he returned, he was wriggling into his jacket, gazing at me sadly, disappointedly.

'I'm going to work,' he said. He moved to the kitchen and spoke through the wire mesh of the door. 'The poor boy must be starving. Can you please give him something to eat?' Then he left, to sit at a desk in the bank next door.

For most of the afternoon, I willed myself to concentrate on playing with their three-year-old, my cousin Sona, under Kuku's powerfully silent supervision, until the shadows began to stretch and I said I was going downstairs. My uncle Jai's house was a slim, three-storey building; its iron double-doors sealed with a chunky foot-long bolt. My bedroom was on the lower floor, along with the bathroom, utility and a further spare room. The rest of the family slept either in the large living room on the middle storey or, if it was especially hot, like now, across charpoys on the roof. I rolled the suitcase into my room, closed the door, drew the curtain across it, and dropped to the bed, lying flat on my back. The ceiling fan whirred, stuck on its lowest setting and creaking with every revolution. The window to my left, twice as high as it was wide, looked out on to one of the bazaar's side lanes. A man was swirling jalebis in a huge black vat of oil. Another man was berating him from the balcony above. I reached across and drew the curtain over the scene, so that my veiled room was suddenly filled with a treacly dark light, reddish-brown, too thick for the air from the fan to penetrate. I could feel my back seeping moisture. I checked my rucksack, more for reassurance than anything else, and, yes, I still had the four bottles of local Bagpiper I'd bought on the twelve-hour coach ride from Delhi. I lay back down. I didn't think I'd need any more alcohol tonight. I'd cushioned myself well enough, I hoped, but it felt good to know it was there. I hadn't had a hit of heroin for twenty-four hours. I was so very frightened of what lay ahead.

Later, I was pacing the room, twitching, already fighting my panic, when Jai arrived with a greasy blue bag of fried chicken, two cans of sweating Coke, and laid it all out at the foot of my bed on a tablecloth he pulled from his rear pocket. Not much was said. We paused in our eating every few minutes and sat absolutely still, as if that might give us some respite from the heat. The four wall lights were all of heavy glass moulded to look like seashells and together they cast a foul glow that seemed almost sulphuric. I picked at the chicken, stripping it of its skin. It tasted bitter. Everything did.

'So how's my big sis and brother-in-law?' Jai asked with forced cheer. 'Any retirement plans yet?'

I shook my head. It hurt to talk too much.

'They'll drop dead behind that counter, those two.'

I nodded, slowly. Some moments passed before Jai went on, more sombrely.

'Ignore your aunt. You know what she's like. But I'm sorry she's kept you hungry.'

'I can go somewhere else if it helps.'

'We rub along well enough most of the time. It can't be easy for her. Married to someone she hates.'

I glanced up at him, swigging his Coke, looking at me over the can. He put the drink back down, shrugged.

'She wanted to marry someone else. What can you do?'

'How do you know she wanted to marry someone else?'

'He was a neighbour from her own village. Which means he might as well have been her brother.' He ran his hand down his face. 'Oh, she told me. The day after the wedding. She told me.'

I looked back down, sad for him, and carried on picking at my food.

'Is her village far?' I asked. I knew nothing about my aunt. On previous visits I'd been too young to pay her any attention, registering her as little more than a sour presence behind the stiff net of the kitchen door.

'Far? It's the next village along! You know our old farm? Half an hour beyond that and you're there.'

I'd forgotten about the farm. I think I'd been there once, as a kid. I have a memory of being carried on the scoop of my mum's hip as she walked around an empty courtyard, smiling to herself.

'Who lives on the farm now?'

'Mosquitoes,' he said, and pinged my can with his thumbnail. 'Drink.'

I nodded. 'Later.'

'You must be tired.'

I nodded again. He seemed to want me to continue, but I didn't, and some more time passed.

'Is everything okay, son?'

'Couldn't be better.'

He looked put out, aggrieved, even, as if I'd gone back on a promise, and I realised he'd only been so honest with me in the hope the intimacy would be returned. I imagined him at his desk all afternoon, calculating how best to get me talking.

'You drank quite a bit earlier.'

'Can I have a blanket, please? I'm—'

'And you don't look well,' he added, before I'd even got my sentence out. 'A blanket? In this furnace?'

We finished the meal in silence, until I said I was full, and Jai, in no great hurry, perhaps fearing the hostility upstairs, bundled the bones and empty cans back into the damp blue bag. He considered the tablecloth for a moment, crushed that into the bag, too, and kissed the top of my head, saying he'd throw a blanket down.

Around midnight, closing the door with care, I slipped back out into the hallway, which was a tall roofless corridor. I remember looking up, at the astonishments of the stars framed by the four high walls. There was the sound of scooters quacking their horns, and from over the gate rich notes of leather and diesel and shit. In the bathroom, I stepped out of my boxers, turned the lever with my shaking hand and stood my sweating body under the steaming water, my shoulders hunched and teeth chattering. I'd forgotten to grab a towel, but drip-dried fast enough, and at the sink outside the bathroom I avoided looking in the mirror as I tipped the tooth-brushes out of the plastic tumbler and took the tumbler back to my room. I poured half a glass of whisky, necked it, and sat doubled-over at the end of the bed, under the slow fan. Its creaking began to bother me as much as any noise ever had, and I got up and slapped frantically at the dial until the thing agreed to stop. Swallowing, scared, I stood with my back to the wall. I thought I'd have had longer before my cluck started, but already I was scratching, at my elbows, my back, my feet. My skin felt as if it was crawling, as if it didn't fit my body. My stomach convulsed, convulsed again, a heaving as hard and dry as a lizard's spine, and at the third retch my hand leapt to my mouth and caught grey slugs of chicken. I drank another whisky, a larger one this time, and then, still freezing, still shivering, I climbed under the blanket.

On the third day, Jai and Kuku entered my room, along with a man I hadn't seen before. It was early afternoon: behind me I could hear kids ambling home from school. I was sitting on the window ledge with my hands pressed under my thighs and my feet lifted to the sweat-marked bed.

'This is Dr Duggal,' Jai said, stepping aside with habit-ual deference. 'We thought he might take a look at you. Just a quick one.'

It felt like the least I could do for my uncle, who was gamely putting up with me living in his house. The doctor, who was elderly and with exactingly side-parted white hair, had an air of having been dragged here against his will. Perhaps he'd just been finishing up for the day. He placed his black medical bag on the bed and took out his stethoscope.

'Lift your arms,' he said. 'Open your mouth – flex your fingers – breathe in – out.'

More instructions followed and I acquiesced to each one, though my joints felt so unlubricated it was as if my bones were grinding up against each other. When he shone a light in my mouth I thought my teeth would fall out on to my tongue. I admitted none of this.

'Dengue,' Dr Duggal said.

'Dengue?' said Jai.

'Dengue.'

'Doctor?' Jai said.

'He's struggling to lift his arms, the temperature, sweating, et cetera. It looks like dengue fever. Nothing to do. Water and rest.'

'If you're sure,' Jai said, though he didn't sound convinced.

'Well.' Dr Duggal looked irritated, unused to having his diagnosis questioned, or, maybe, these days, sick of it. 'Have there been any other symptoms?'

I shook my head.

'If it gets worse, take him to the city hospital.'

Jai turned away from me, as if wishing to speak to the doctor privately. 'He has soiled himself a few times.'

'Speak up. I left my aid.'

'He shat himself,' Kuku supplied, enunciating very clearly.

Dr Duggal looked to his bag on my bed, then moved it to the floor.

'Should he even be in this house?' Kuku shot me a poisonous look. 'My poor son. All this time he's been exposed to this disease. Shouldn't he' – meaning me – 'go somewhere else?'

'I don't see a rash, Doctor,' said another voice.

I'd had a sense that someone else was in the room. She'd been standing far back, obscured by shadows, and now moved a little forward. With both hands, she held her own medical bag down in front of her skirt, which was floor-length, pleated. Over her white blouse she wore a short doctor's coat, light blue instead of white. She seemed to be levitating, gliding towards me. I couldn't tell how old she was.

'How's his sleep?'

'He's not sleeping at all,' Jai said enthusiastically, as if this younger doctor might be on to something. 'I can hear him pacing about, turning the fan on and off all the time, sometimes too hot, sometimes too cold. He's always going to the toilet.'

'A rash isn't as common as your manuals would have you believe,' Dr Duggal said.

'And he's been like this since the day he arrived?' the younger doctor asked.

'Via Delhi,' Dr Duggal said, as though that settled things. 'Awful epidemic of dengue in that city. He's been most unlucky. Most unfortunate.'

I saw her looking at my clothes. 'It's very hot to be wearing a jumper,' she observed.

'He's always shaking,' Jai said. 'Is that normal with dengue?'

'Mentally, any ... bad thoughts?' she asked, this time to me.

'Who's the senior in charge here?' Dr Duggal said, glancing around the room in a show of sarcasm, but she continued looking at me intently, until at last she conceded the ground and let him take over once more.

The first time I left the house was to use the telephone. The aching by then was mostly concentrated in my shins and I could control that by walking on my heels and only very gently pressing down on to the balls of my feet. I had a shower, changed into a fleece because the shivering was still inside me, and called up to my uncle, whose face now appeared over the terraced railing.

'I'm just going to the PCO.'

'Oh.' He looked surprised, then cautiously happy. 'Feeling better?'

'I won't be long.'

'Take your time. Some fresh air, that's what you need. Are you calling home? Do you want some money? Won't you be hot?'

'I won't be long,' I repeated and stepped through the door-shaped hatch in the iron gate, fists in my pockets, heading for the bazaar. It was strange moving from painfully bright sunlight into the darker lanes of the market, where the sun felt unwelcome and everything seemed touched by loss. A great despondency hit me, like sand slowing me down, and I stopped and sat on some stone steps and closed my eyes. I thought of how on previous visits I'd loved walking around the bazaar, enjoying the feeling of looking like everyone else for a change, but now all I wanted was to be free from all this.

'Which country?' the woman at the PCO asked, little able to disguise her boredom.

'England, please,' and after pressing some buttons on her switchboard, she bowed her head ironically – 'Mister England' – and invited me to take the final cubicle in the row.

My dad answered and somehow I hadn't been prepared for his gentle, deep hello, the way it closed something in my throat.

'How are you, son?'

I nodded, kept nodding.

'I know,' he said, as if he could see me.

'It's hot, Dad.' *I love you, Dad.*

'I know, son.'

He'd had to come pick me up one night a few weeks ago, when I'd spent all my money on scoring and just had enough left to use a payphone. It was a wet night, I remember, water streaming down the windscreen, and as we paused at a fuzzy ruby traffic light, he asked me what plans I had for the summer.

I was leaning far back in my seat, worrying I'd not scored enough for the next day. 'I'll need things for uni. A lamp and stuff. I can get them tomorrow,' I added sheepishly. 'If you give me some money.'

He turned to the window, away from me. 'Your mum and I thought you could go to your uncle. In India. Get away from everything here.'

'I don't know.' I didn't want to talk about it. 'Probably not.'

I saw him nod. 'We can't force you. Everyone tells me it has to be your choice.' I heard him breathe out, as if expelling all the air inside him. 'It's like we're not allowed to help you.'

I didn't say anything. I was finding it hard to process the idea that my dad had resorted to searching out doctors, experts, about his son's drug habit.

When we got home, he paused outside the door, touched my arm, and said he'd take some time off tomorrow and come shopping with me to buy whatever I needed to start uni.

I nodded.

'Please,' he said, as if unable to help himself.

'Don't say please,' I replied, so quietly, so very glad of the rain.

When I arrived back at my uncle's house, I could hear Jai on the terrace but see only his shadow mounting the concrete wall. He was on the phone and appeared to have his hand cupping the back of his head, or maybe his neck. I carried on into my room and pulled out my rucksack, the empty bottles of Bagpiper rattling about inside. There was barely half a plastic tumbler's worth between them. I heard Jai coming down the stairs.

'How's the family?' he asked, as I zipped up the rucksack and kicked it back under the bed. He looked excited, full of impatience.

'Good. Everything's good. I might get myself something to eat in a bit.'

'There's some carrot-thing in the fridge. Help yourself. You do look better.'

'I'm sorry for worrying you, Uncle. Thank you for taking care of me.'

He batted the gratitude away and said all he'd done was give me a roof under which to beat the fever. 'But I need to nip next door and then go see a client in Kapurthala. Finally some proper responsibility!' He jiggled his wrist to get a look at his watch. 'Your aunt's out shopping ...'

I said nothing. Though I knew I should, I didn't want to keep an eye on my cousin Sona. I wanted to head to the liquor store.

'She'll be back any minute now, I'm sure. Just sit with him?'

I smiled. 'Of course.'

'You'll be okay?' He sounded uncertain himself now, which goaded me.

'We'll be fine,' and after seeing him out the gate, I ascended the stairs, heel to toe, heel to toe, flinching with every step, and found my cousin sprawled across the huge bed in the living room, absorbed in a Hindi-dubbed version of *Scooby-Doo*. The fan stirred the hems of his camo-shorts.

I sat on the end of the bed, which was high enough to leave my feet dangling, and I kept drumming my heels together, anxiously, impatiently. She'll be back any minute now. Any minute now. Any minute. Now. She wasn't.

'Don't make noise,' Sona said, eyes tight on the screen, and I apologised and brought my knees up to my chin, tidying my feet away underneath myself. But that flared up some of the joint pain from the previous week and all at once I stood up.

'We're going out.'

As promised, I gave him a piggyback, but within a couple of minutes he became as heavy as a horse and I had to persuade him to walk. He wasn't fat, far from it, I simply had no strength. The bazaar was busy, mazy, and I felt his hand slip into mine as I tunnelled through. He didn't say anything. He was quite an inward child, inevitably, perhaps, in the unhappy atmosphere of that house. Once through the bazaar, the ferocious heat hit us and the sun smashed into the white dome of the Sikh temple. I felt it as shards of painful light. The asphalt of the road was giving off rags of steam.

'This way,' I said, already pulling him along the sandy verge.

'Are we nearly there?'

'Yes, yes,' I told him, though it was still several minutes of walking away. All the liquor stores were commanded to keep to the village boundary, away from ordinary decent folk.

When we arrived I seated Sona on a concrete step in the thin shade of the wall, promising him an ice cream on the way back. I approached the grilled window, where the string-vested owner, I'll never forget, was blinded in one eye. The eyeball was entirely white, pearlescent, save for two streaks of a very delicate red, like crosshairs. I asked for a peg of his cheapest and he handed it to me through the hatch. It smelled of vinegar and tasted worse, but it blunted my edges and slowed down my running, jerking mind.

'Englandia?' he said, when I asked to buy three bottles of the stuff.

I nodded.

'Where from you? I have family in Madeyhead.' Maidenhead. I thought it strange that he'd switched to English when I'd been speaking smooth Punjabi to him beforehand. It was only later that I realised my speech during my entire withdrawal had been kicking off with a stammer, the sounds of a man whose body is in sharp revolt.

'The north.'

'Manchester?'

'Aberdeen,' I lied, to make the conversation stop.

'Oh, I know Aberdeen! I work in Torry little time. Where you live?'

I mumbled something about being near the football ground and before he could ask me which one, I grabbed my bag of jangling bottles and turned down the side of the store, where Sona had nodded off.

'Come on, dude,' I said.

His arms were crossed over his small knees, and his head rested in the cushioned bend of his elbow. I put the bag down and lifted his face to mine, saying his name. His face had paled, he seemed floppy, wavy, his features zoned out and puddled. I screamed for water, for help, as my heart raced in an awful way.

All evening, shut away in my room, I could hear my aunt shouting and my uncle trying desperately to calm her down, or at any rate to get her to lower her voice. The whole bazaar could hear.

'Let them! Maybe someone out there can be the man you're not. I knew I'd been married off to a fool, but I thought even you would have the sense not to put your son in danger.'

'Kuku, please be sensible. What on earth will my sister think if I ask him to leave?'

'Come look, everyone! Pity me, the wife of a eunuch! My foot slipped into the grave when I was married off to him!'

'Kuku, you're reaching my limit. Now please stop.'

'Don't you dare put your hands on me! Don't you ever touch me!'

'I'm your husband. I demand you show me that respect.'

I flinched then, hearing a crack, and a collective gasp from onlookers gathered at the mouth of the bazaar. She would have slapped him, I knew that.

By the time he came down the stairs, I'd packed my suitcase and had it ready at the foot of the bed, my rucksack resting on top.

'You don't have to go anywhere.'

His eyes were the scrubbed red of someone who'd been crying and, dear lord, I wished there was something else I could do. I hooked up my rucksack. 'I'm so sorry I didn't look after Sona. I don't know what else to say.'

'Duggal says he'll be fine. Mild sunstroke, nothing more. But don't go, son. Please. She'll calm down by the morning. I know what she's like.'

'I'll call home tomorrow and let them know where I am. I'll explain everything. Don't worry.'

'But where will you go? This is silly!'

'I thought the farm? If it's okay with you, can I go there?' I'd been thinking about the place ever since he'd reminded me of it.

He scrunched his brow, as if it took him a moment to work out which farm I meant. 'Of course you can't! There's nothing there. On your own! How will you even eat?'

I moved past him, wedging the door open with my foot as I waggled my case through, wheeling it across the uncovered passageway. I stopped at the gate to hug him.

'Let's call your parents,' he said, breaking off the embrace.

'I'm going to the farm.'

'But why!'

'The quiet. It'll help me get better.' I was craving solitude. 'It's only a few weeks. I am eighteen, you know.'

'Old enough to be beyond this stubbornness. So much like your mother.'

I had made it out into the bazaar, wondering who to ask for directions, when he called my name. I waited, making a visor of my hand, and watched him approach, his face growing more resigned with every step.

'Once you're over this fever-thing, you come straight back, yes?'

'We'll see.'

He shook his head. 'Let me get us a car.'

He borrowed a bank colleague's battered white Maruti and sat in the passenger seat, directing me on to the back road, past the Hindu shrines and the swamp, and out to a narrow and gruelling path through some wheat fields. The car had zero suspension and I worried for my bottles in the rucksack. The family farm, he told me, over the rattling havoc of the air-con, was nearly three kilometres from the house and had lain empty for many years, ever since they'd built the house in the village proper.

'Stop here,' he said, and I braked, though we were still on the path, with no farm – or any other building, for that matter – in sight. 'Walking time,' he explained, which was no real explanation.

A little up ahead, we took a turning into such deep red sand that my trainers sank an inch with every step. I started to see a building, at first obscured by large plane trees, but then slowly, with a quality almost of shyness, it crept into view. It looked silent, neglected, all exposed yellow brick. The wheels of my case trailed snake-lines behind us, which disturbed me strangely, a feeling as if I was being followed, even watched, but when I turned back to face the house I felt an intimation that something here had been patiently waiting for years. Getting closer, I noticed patches of pale pink clinging to the yellow brickwork, and a blue barrel hovering as if in mid-air that had maybe once been a water tank. We came to a warped iron gate secured by a metal chain and a brass padlock as big as my palm.

'But anyone could climb over, right?' I said, moving to the wall, which was no higher than my head.

I stood on my case and pulled myself up, my arms shaking with the strain. The drop on the other side was broken into two easy steps thanks to a large stone bath, empty and carpeted in soft green moss. I was in a court-yard of hard, compacted earth, the colour of peanuts, and in front of me the homestead curved round like a horse-shoe, with its flat roof and its pillars of peeling paint. There looked to be some rooms at the back of the porch. I could make out darkened door-shapes, and to the sides as well, the left one seemingly a barn leading on to what-ever was at the rear of the house. The room to my right, sitting apart from the main building, had a window, iron-barred. Jai landed beside me, just missing the water pump.

'I'll call a locksmith over tomorrow.' He glanced around, looking depressed by what he saw. 'Change your mind? It's not too late.'

'Let's see how it goes.'

He took a step forward and became animated, spreading his arms out wide. 'I used to play cricket in this courtyard, you know. When I was little. All the time!' By degrees, his grin dwindled. I imagine he felt a pang, a sadness for the dreamy boy who knew nothing of the sad little man he would become, because suddenly he seemed desperate to leave.

'I should give the car back. Or shall I show you round?'

'I'll be fine. Thank you.'

'I'll send a boy round with a tiffin each day. If you want to get hold of me, just let him know. Is there anything else you need?'

In one corner of the yard, pointedly away from the house, was a lopsided wooden cubicle. 'Is that the toilet?'

'Hmm? Oh, yes. But,' he went on after a moment, perhaps remembering the constant shitting of the previous days, 'we should have picked up some toilet paper. I'll send some with the boy tomorrow. But it's an old-style one, this toilet. Hand-flushing.'

I worked the water pump, which still drew, albeit fitfully. 'No worries.'

'If it dries up, maybe try starting the well?' He sounded unsure; he was a man with no practical ability, and I didn't want to embarrass him by asking how I'd actually do that, so I simply nodded, and said I was sure it'd be fine. He seemed to sense my pity, because he said, a little viciously, 'Surely a lucky foreign boy like you can work it out?'

He climbed back over the wall, fumblingly threw my case over to me, and without much of a shout goodbye he got into the car. I heard him stall the engine twice, then finally get it going, and I stood there, my ears full of the car withdrawing, long after Jai would have reached his house, parked up and rejoined his wife.

Night came all at once, like a cupboard door shutting, and I heaved out a charpoy, its frame cracked and loose and showing signs of woodworm, its weave so slack that it was more hammock than bed. I couldn't find any utensils, no beaker or plate, and I didn't want to drink neat from the bottle. I needed to make it last. So I unscrewed the top with its desi logo, poured a thimbleful of whisky and added water from the pump. It felt totally incongruous, trying to subdue my body's cravings by sipping whisky with such daintiness, thumb and forefinger only, like one of those Chinese emperors and their miniature cups of tea.

The moon was out, a button of light, and the stars shone dully. I'd switched my jumper for a T-shirt and felt a small breeze crawl off the surrounding fields and across my skin. I was sitting awkwardly, my elbows bent on my knees in a way that hid the undersides of my forearms. Beyond the wall, the plane trees were black and frighteningly tall. My phone was at my side. There was no signal, of course, but the green light was useful. I wasn't sure how I'd cope once it died. And maybe it was the light that attracted the mosquitoes, because soon enough they came for me, one by one at first, and then a near swarm biting my legs. They find foreign, whiter flesh sweeter, I'd been told many times, as if I were an apple beneath their keen little teeth. I stood, slapping at my arms, my neck, scratching at my calf with the heel of my other leg. They forced me into the porch, and there I sat with my back against a pillar, the bottle on the floor.

I drank five more thimblefuls, neat, then, fortified, decided to see what was beyond each of the three doors. None of them were locked and I went from room to room: charpoys strewn here and there; an old-looking cupboard, the oval mirror cracked, the whole silver-webbed and filthy. Empty metal chests. More charpoys. Some earthenware inkpots. A hookah with a deflated balloon attached to its pipe. A child's cot, one side of it broken. A few tins of Ovaltine and a small pile of animal bones. There was a hole smashed low into a wall and, tilting my phone face down, I saw that the greenlit floors were splattered with animal shit.

Back outside, I dragged my charpoy-hammock from the courtyard and dropped it under the porch. I'd just have to stay here. I didn't think I'd need any more alcohol. Things felt nicely muddled, though complicated by waves of guilt over Sona. How stupid. Selfish and stupid. I lay flat on my back and the muscles in my stomach strained, a hurt that felt closer to pleasure because the cramps had started to soften out. I thought I might even get some sleep, that perhaps the new surroundings were helping. But just as my eyes were beginning to close, bats flared out of one of the rooms; I covered my face and felt a rush of furred and flapping air as the excited colony swooped over me. Shaken, I got to my feet and had another swig of whisky, this time straight from the bottle. No, I didn't want to sleep in the porch. A toad croaked somewhere in the fields. Was there anyone between me and the main village? How far was it – about as far as the town centre was from the shop back home? Not that far, but enough to feel very alone; enough to feel as if that was all the world there was and would ever be. I considered my options. The barn stank of peat and sulphur. The only other room was the small one with the iron-barred window, adjacent to the porch but not part of it. Three bolts, deep in rust, ran across the top, middle and bottom of the door, and however hard I tried they wouldn't give. Behind the room, though, a set of stairs led to the roof. I carried my charpoy and my cheap whisky up and stood there, alone, on the roof of a nameless farm beyond the outskirts of a village that was, in turn, at least a twelve-hour drive from the nearest city anyone would have heard of.

I got some sleep to begin with, that night, though I wasn't sure how much because at some point my phone died. The cramps and the dry heaving and the shin pains then restarted, not debilitatingly, nor even painfully compared with what had already passed, but enough to prevent any further rest. I hauled myself from the sagging well of a bed and swung my legs on to the ground, which was still warm with heat. I'd just have to push through these nights. There couldn't be many more of them; surely soon my body would let me be? For the hell of it, I stretched myself out along the very rim of the charpoy's frame, balancing my long, thin body in line with the wooden beam, pushed up on to my hand, and counted. It was a game I'd played on previous trips to India, when the noonday sun would compel us all inside. Back then, I could count to well over 100, but now I hadn't even made it to double digits when my strength gave and my elbow buckled and I and the cot collapsed. Laughing, I moved to the low wall that edged the roof. What was I doing here? This place held the kind of silence that could send a man mad. A brooding, hot, paranoid, creeping silence, full of imagined sounds and nothing noises: was that the creak of a tree or a tiger's low growl? A gurgle of the water tank or a viper's approaching rattle?

As the night started to lift, it left a lead-grey mistiness hanging over the unhedged fields. In the distance, among the wheat, were greener shapes; I knew them to be rect-angles of paddy and local rice but from where I was stand-ing they appeared as green and as flat as any field in England. I could see myself running through those fields, twelve years old; I could see the green on my estate and myself running to my friend's house with fluttery excitement in my stomach. I wore a lilac Ben Sherman shirt, which I untucked as soon as I exited our shop, and in my hand was an enveloped birthday card with ten pounds folded inside it. At the pub, I turned right on to the main road and up the steep hill. I hated walking up this road, or up any road round here. I was always being stared at, my presence noted and remarked upon for its rarity in this town. My head was down. I refused to look up. I can't remember ever looking up as a child without immediately feeling as if I had no right and should look away. I turned right again, down an alley, and a few moments later walked up a concrete path and knocked on a side entrance of corrugated plastic, because no one ever used their front doors. I checked my collar – look neat, look neat – and saw a big shape approach, blurred as a bear until the door opened. It was Spencer's dad. I'd never met him before but over time I came to learn that he was a former miner who now stacked shelves in Morrisons. He only did nights, because he couldn't face the public shame of being reduced to that line of work. Every other Saturday he forwent his own lunch and dinner so he might still afford to take his sons to the football. A deeply proud man brought to his bitter knees. Fifteen years later, dementia-raddled, all he'd talk about were his friends down the pit. But none of that could mean a thing to a twelve-year-old boy horribly aware of what was signalled by the change in this man's face when he pulled open the door.

'Hello,' I said, and I can still remember how hard and fearfully my heart was thudding. 'Spencer's party?' The door opened straight into the kitchen and, behind Spencer's dad, I could see some of my classmates and their parents, chatting, drinking pop, hair newly curled.

'Let him in, love,' said a woman, Spencer's mum, with something tremulous in her voice.

'I'm sorry,' Spencer's dad said, to me. 'No.'

Everyone inside went silent. Spencer's mum managed a laugh. 'You can't turn him away.'

'I can do what I like, my love. It's my own house.' To me: 'There'll be no need to come here again.'

He nodded in a way that made me nod too, as if I were somehow complicit, and then he closed the door. I made it off the drive, embarrassed, stinking with shame, when footsteps came puttering up behind me. The mum. She had a soft, loose face and a tired blonde perm.

'Pay it no mind, will you. He should know better at his age.' She passed me a small purple bag, glossy and bright with stars. 'Some cake.' And I passed her the envelope, the card with ten pounds folded inside it. I don't know why. The need to complete an exchange, perhaps. But, really, looking back, I think I was simply thanking her, for letting me know that what just happened wasn't my fault, that it was not deserved, though I felt as if it was and that it must have been.

One midnight four years later, out of my face on smack, I'd launch half a brick through their front window, but back then, the cake-bag in my hand, I went to Ringwood Park, over the main road. I dangled on the swings for a while, chains grating metal on metal, eating my cake, and then followed the BMX track round to where some steps led up to a field, and then to a large beautiful grotty lake. I took a slow walk round, stopping now and then to smile at the spotty yellow fish, and in those moments forgetting about Spencer and his party, and after completing two circuits of the water I made for home, entering the shop to see my dad at the counter.

'Party over? Did you have fun?'

There was hope in his voice along with a note of worry, and he looked relieved when I said, 'Great. I should have saved you some cake.'

I came through the counter-flap and we low-fived. It was kind of a family rule that whenever I returned home from somewhere, say from school or from delivering the papers, from anywhere really, I first acknowledged my parents with an embrace, unless a customer was present, when a touching of hands would do. I never saw any of my cousins' families in Derby or Birmingham or Southall act like this and, as I got older, I wondered if the gesture was my parents' way of saying that I was home now, with them, that I was safe, or at least safer, because it was always impossible to feel at ease in that place, where public displays of violence were only ever a door-chime away.

'First time he's been invited to a friend's house,' I heard Dad explaining, as I went through into the back and up the stairs.

I watched the boy in the distant field climbing the stairs to his room, embracing his mother on the way, who's also excited to know how the party went, and then I sighed and looked down, surprised to see a small brown wasteland at the back of the farm. It was a walled rectangle, mudded over and desolate. In the far wall, some bricks stuck out, footholds to aid climbing, and in the top right corner grew a single peepal tree, a gangly reedy unhappy thing. A pen for the animals, back in the day? I lifted the charpoy on to my back and carried it down the stairs, cursing as I went. Then I got ready, washing my face at the pump, brushing my teeth in the middle of the yard, filled with a sudden morning sense of freedom, of hope, that I was here, with the run of the farm on a day as bright as parrots, free to do whatever I wanted. I took a piss in the latrine, changed, and then shoved the charpoy into a shady spot near the barn and caught up on some sleep, woken a few hours later by tiny stones showering down on me. Groggily, I realised they were coming from over the wall.

'Fuck's sake,' I shouted, in English, getting up. 'What's your problem?'

'No problem!' His voice shrilled. 'I'm Laxman. I've got your tiffin and ... wiping tissues?'

I climbed up on to the stone bath and peered over the wall. He smiled. He had large eyes and about three teeth. And he wasn't a boy like Jai had said but a barefoot white-bearded man in wide olive trousers and a black hand-me-down *Ghostbusters* T-shirt that I imagine he'd politely accepted from some visiting Californian relative. He passed up the food and the bog roll, a torch and some soap, too, and I wondered if I was meant to tip him, whether he'd be offended if I saved my money and didn't, when he said the job shouldn't take him long. I must have looked nonplussed because he pointed to his basket of tools, which he'd left at the gate.

'I'll have to break the chain and put on a new lock. Really, the whole gate needs replacing. You can get good ones now, single, double, side-panel, steel tubing, wrought iron, iron scrolls. Lots of choice at Shankar and Sons in the city.'

'I'll tell my uncle.'

'Tell, yes. And if you tell them I sent you I get ten per cent.'

He shuffled off towards his tools and I returned to my charpoy, separated out the tiffin's steel bowls, left some food aside for later, and ate the lentil daal. There was an elephant sticker on the side of one of the bowls: 'Eat at Dimple's Dhaba'. So my uncle had instructed one of the local street joints to sort out my meals: my aunt must have refused. I couldn't blame her. When the gate opened, the hinges objecting mightily, I left my food and walked over to Laxman.

'That's great,' I said. 'Thanks for coming.'

'I've not done anything yet. Only broken the chain.'

I hadn't been subtle – I wanted solitude – but he was aggrieved. Roughly he removed the old rusted locks and drilled a fresh hole in the wall, securing a new bolt, and came over only once he'd finished, weighed down by the basket of tools in one oily hand. I was at the guava tree near the barn, snapping off the fruit, slicing it in my palm. I offered him a piece. He looked away.

'Then let me give you something,' I said, wallet at the ready.

'You are young enough to be my grandson. I'll speak to your uncle.'

I nodded, chastened.

'Leave the tiffin outside the gate when you're finished and someone in my family will collect it each morning. They'll leave behind the new one. Is that clear?'

I nodded again and then he grunted and turned to go. He was beyond the gate when I called for him to stop. I'd remembered the little room, the rusted bolts.

'What is it?' he said, stubbornly remaining where he was.

I jogged over. 'Could you open that room there as well? The bolts are stuck.'

We walked to the door together, past the iron bars of the window and the rectangle of wood that covered it up from the inside.

'Why do you want to be opening up this old room?'

'To sleep in. The mosquitoes love me round here.'

He seemed reluctant, his mouth pursed.

'It's not a big job, is it?' I asked, confused. Maybe it was a special room of some sort, used for prayers and offerings. 'Is it a baba room?'

'You're your uncle's real nephew, yes? Not some side-cousin's boy?'

'Yeah,' I replied, warily, because he knew that already and so his question must really have been about something else.

'Mehar Kaur's blood?'

I was pulled up short by his use of her name. In India, the nature of the relationship always comes first.

'She was my great-grandmother,' I said.

He nodded thoughtfully, looking at me the whole time, running his eyes so hard over my face that I felt forced to turn away. 'Is this her room? Is that what you're saying?' When he didn't respond I touched the bars and noticed that none of the other windows were closed off in this way. 'You knew her?'

'I think I saw her once or twice, when I was young and cycling past. She was getting old by then.'

And without another word he sized up the locks, took a couple of hammers from his tool-basket and passed one to me. Being taller, I started on the top bolt.

8

Riding his mule, it takes Jeet an age to force his way through the hedge of dawdling city-folk and through the old clay arch. Things aren't much better inside the city bazaar, where the crabby lanes teem and the blue hoardings shed so much dust that he shades the animal's eyes with his own hand. *Bata Sandals Many Price. Hira Mandi. Best Rate Furniture. Phagwara Number 1 Royal Fabric Palace* (this last hoarding always odd, in Jalandhar, a good half-day's ride from the small town of Phagwara). Rickshaws jangle by, wheels turning, and through their spokes Jeet glimpses a fat old man in a long Kashmiri kurta, lounging about in an open porch and puffing on his long green hookah, letting the world know he'd been to the courtesans above. Decadent fool.

He really does hate cities, Jeet thinks, and the people who live in them. Or maybe, he wonders, adjusts, it is simply that he appreciates his village more. Simply. Yes, he thinks on, his thoughts not quite staying in lane, that must be how these people look on him and his village: its simple roads and houses; his simple farm and life. His simple wife. She would appear so simple to these rich city women, with their lacy fans and their faces not even half covered. But only he knows of the intelligence in his wife's eyes, and only he will ever know: a realisation that radiates a pulse of arousal through his body.

He is always watching her. He's shifted his charpoy a foot along the wall so that when he wakes he can lie there, one eye to the crack in the wood, and spy her stepping from room to pump, the weak morning light coming off her sleeves as her hands render the animal fat to soap. There was a moment the previous week when, breathing hard, he stopped threshing, threw aside the flail, and told the other men he was going for a shit. Instead, he moved closer to the road because he knew she'd be on her way to the temple and he needed to see her. He was watching her pass by, the tiffin in her hands, when she dropped the tin and bent over. Jeet felt a very precise fear rise in him, a fear of losing her; he could imagine her eyes behind the veil, bulging in their startled hollows. He hurried towards her, jumping through the wheat like some mad hurdler, but one of the others – Harbans – gave three good whacks to her back and they picked up the tin and carried on up the path. He stood there watching them round the bend, a hand to his forehead, relieved and panting and silently imploring the world, God, always to take care of her at times like these, at times when he wasn't around.

He strokes the head of the mule, making two furrows in its brown coat, and yanks the left rein. If neither of his brothers has requested the back room, he'll have a word with Mai as soon as he gets home. Chances are she'll look at him askance – two nights in a row? – and perhaps even shake her head, like she does when the girl is bleeding, but he'll insist. She is his. Joy and pride swell his chest and he leans forward over the animal, folds back its ear and kisses the soft inner pink. What a beautiful day. Sunshine spots the bushes sprouting from the red half-timbered façades. New fretwork gleams above the post office. Wonder when they did that? A horse nips at the yellow skirt of an oblivious white girl while her panicking ayah rushes over with an ice cream. Four men, heads dropped low, play chess in the shade of a lonely minaret. *Naujhawana Ka Dhaba. Watch Repairs. Shahalmi Gate.* Gathering the rein into his fist, he tugs it again, hits the mule with his heel and they veer left at the fork. The lanes are wider here, avenues almost, and he relaxes and breathes the greener air (then coughs out the dust). He tucks in the loose end of his turban and rights his collar just so but when a woman in a pea-green sari gives him a snooty look he petulantly pops his collar back up and kicks his mule on. Left at *Nadira Emporium*, around the throng baiting a dancing bear and on to *Shahbaz Jewellers*, its frilled awning following the lazy curve of the street corner. He stays his mule, hitching it to a melon-cart, and enters the shop. The owner spits betel juice into a spittoon and wipes his red lips in an upward motion with the heel of his hand.

'If you want food go steal from the mandi.' Then, going back to his tobacco pouch: 'Village fools.'

Jeet doesn't blame him. A twenty-two-year-old looking as he does. How is the man to know of the money Mai saved from the three dowries, money she had that dawn brought out from the locked cupboard and placed into his hands? He extracts the wad from his tunic's top pocket and holds it up, as if taking an oath. He thinks of Mehar's face.

'Show me some pearls.'

Exiting the bazaar, passing the officers' cricket ground, the pearls bagged up and tied around his neck, he notices a crowd gathered outside the station. Men in white tunics, their heads covered. A funeral? Here? Jeet mumbles a prayer and, still on his mule, leans down.

'Everything okay, brother?'

'We're mourning the death of our nation,' the man says.

He understands. 'Yes. We all feel it—'

'No need to tell me. They rob us all. Come join us. Sit.'

Jeet hesitates a moment then rises back up on to his mule, the sun crashing into his face.

Banners, green on brown, in both languages: *We are the Freedom Movement!* and *Free India!* Was that an order or a hope for the future? Jeet smiles, then winds the smile in, checks no one saw. Flags, too. It all seems at odds with the peaceful way the men are sitting on the ground, packed tight, hands threaded around raised knees like educated types at dinner. He does want to join them, sit alongside them and their fancy ways, maybe even learn a phrase of English to whisper to Mehar. How strange, he thinks, how new the feeling that he should want to impress her, to have her approval and praise. Humble Jeet, who has always tried never to ask anything of anyone. But he has to go. The pearls, in their velvet purple bag. Smiling again, shaking his head, he squeezes his thighs and turns the animal haltingly around.

Two hours later and Jeet is coming back down the red track to the farm, the mule's hooves muzzled by sand, its tired head lolling low. The sun too is low behind the house, silvering the black crows lined up on the roof and running long shadows along the ground, as though the farm were stretching to meet him. The new tank, he is pleased to note, sits strong on its high wooden perch, piping water on to the steaming buffalo. Should it be closer to the trough, he wonders, when he sees a shape outside the arched entrance, and frowns. It is Suraj, his youngest brother, twenty and hopelessly workshy. He is lying on his charpoy, beard unoiled, shirt untucked, a reed of wheat barely hanging from his mouth. Eyes closed. Jeet dismounts.

'Working hard, I see.'

'Hmm. How was the city?'

'I should ask you. I keep hearing you're there a lot.'
Going brothel to brothel, he doesn't add.

Suraj smiles, lids still closed, and far from anger, or even indignation, it is tenderness that Jeet feels. Unlike their mother, he doesn't see his younger brother as dissolute, as lacking in application, or if he does, he also acknowledges the neglect behind it, the neglect that comes with being the youngest in a world where the eldest commands all. Can change all. Can even change what had been already promised. A stab of guilt, swift, and Jeet unties the velvet bag from his neck.

'Look what I got.'

The lashes part and two lids peel back, eyes resisting the light. 'You got them, then,' Suraj says.

'Do you want to see?'

'They're yours.'

'They're ours.' And, as if to prove it: 'Give them to Mai? He's about to drop dead,' he adds, meaning the mule.

Grabbing up a bucket, Jeet drags the animal round to the tank and, left alone, Suraj removes the jewels from their bag. The strung beads slip as easily as silk through his fingers. Ours, you say? In another life, maybe. He throws the pearls in the air, so high that he has enough time to jump off the cot and stand before catching them. He pockets the emptied bag: it should fetch a few rupees, at least. Then he walks through the arch and into the courtyard, the pearls swinging, wondering if either of his brothers has asked to use the room tonight, though can he really even be bothered with her? All bone, she is. The firewood leans tall in the corner. Why hadn't he chopped it? He'd definitely intended to. He approaches Mai, resting, back to him, on her charpoy in the shade of the wall.

Get up, he'd usually say, as if she were no more than one of the women working in the tannery, but something of the warmth Jeet cast still sits upon him, and he says, softly, 'Mai, I've something for you. From Jeet.'

He holds the pearls across his stretched palm and each bead glows. Mai rolls towards him, the weaves groaning underneath her. She reaches up for the pearls and drops them down her front.

'No more?' she says.

'I haven't stolen any, if that's your thought.'

'Not unheard of, though, is it?'

The sun sinks a little and perhaps that accounts for the chill at his heart.

'Firewood,' she reminds him.

'You've hands,' Suraj shoots back.

A few moments earlier and Mehar is scouring the room for a spool of black thread when she vaguely registers that one of the men has entered the yard. She moves to the window and holds down a lacquered slat. Something catches the light. Pearls! She is sure of it. Pearls swinging from his hand. Her husband spoke of pearls. Her heart surges and her gaze lifts to take in his face. She looks at the prominent set of his cheeks, the light stubble that (as far as she can see) gives way to a thicker, if not exactly thick, beard. His mischievous eyes and their ridiculously fine lashes. The sloping set of his shoulders. Yes, she tells herself, the contours of him exactly match the shape of the man who visits her at night. His height, his legs. She knows, of course, about what goes on *between* his legs, and for the first time this thought, coupled with him standing as if naked in his own sun, blooms deep arousal in the roots of her. Her eyes follow him, see him approach Mai, and then she closes the slat, sits on her bed and, her mind careering, reaches for her pillow and buries her beaming face in it.

9

A whole day passes and Mehar hasn't told anyone of what she's discovered. Not even Harbans, who expresses affection so easily and to whom Mehar feels closest. In this house where she is afforded no independence of mind, it feels mutinous to hold her new knowledge close, mutinous and necessary. Mehar smiles. She is with her sisters at the window of the china room, awaiting their summons and watching the brothers. Still she doesn't let on that the man on the right, sitting on the ground a few feet from the other two, one knee pitched up, the other lying flat, is hers. He spoons the saag directly on to his roti, his fingers long and fine. She can't believe that she ever thought the brothers alike, now that she can really see him. What a noble face he has. Oh, Lord, hurry the night when we are together.

'Mai's not tapped any of us for tonight yet, has she?' Mehar tries, oh-so-casually.

'Thank god!' replies Harbans.

'Look who's getting itchy!' Gurleen says, in a breezy tone that trails an undeniable chill.

Mehar, about to reply, thinks better of it and they wait in silence until the brothers leave the yard. The three women file out and collect the dirty dishes. Mehar makes a beeline for the rightmost bowl.

10

Later, Mai having given the nod, Mehar lies on the charpoy in the back room, smiling to herself, her pulse so
strong she can hear the blood in her ears. The door rattles
open and she jumps, then licks her fingers to smooth a
few hairs from her forehead, which is a vanity, given the
complete absence of light. She feels him sitting down at
the end of the bed, by her left foot, and a lovely buzz
travels up her calf, a feeling she hasn't experienced before.

'You are well?' he asks.

She nods, then, 'Yes.'

There's a noise, a soft tapping, and something cold
lands against her arm.

'I said about the pearls.'

'Yes.'

'I don't know if you believe in it or not but now we have
them you might as well put them under the pillow.'

'Yes,' and she takes the necklace up, stringed moons in the dark, and stows it under the pillow, behind her head. The fact that he'd allowed for, or at least considered, her belief (or not) emboldens her to risk saying something more: 'And you? You are well?'

He is quiet and her stomach dips – she shouldn't have said anything! He thinks her loose! – but then: 'Vandals are after our lands. I'm sleeping out a lot. Bad times. These are bad times.'

Mehar knows nothing of this. Nothing of the news that in parts of the country and of the state, in fact, not more than ten miles from her room, many thousands have died in sectarian riots fanned by the publication of *Rangila Rasul*. She knows nothing of the necklaces of shoes some Muslims are being made to wear, nothing of the banning of foreign cloth, or that the drumbeats she sometimes hears at night are a signal to the British that their time is coming to an end.

She feels him stand and when she hears him stepping out of his underwear she begins untying her salwar.

Once he begins, she does something that she's never dared before. She places her hands across his back. He makes a noise like a groan, but she can tell it's a sound of deep pleasure, so she presses her hands harder into his skin and the faster he gets the more she presses, the more she thinks of his face at the side of her neck, his beautiful confident face here with her. Her mind shimmers and she floods with some uncontrollable feeling until all she can do to stop from crying out is bite into his naked shoulder.

11

In so many ways she has brought lightness to the house. The way she breaks off some jaggery when she thinks no one is looking. How perfectly she mimics Mai behind her back. That she persuades Harbans to play hopscotch on the roof, kissing Gurleen, who threatens to inform on them. Her sheer liveliness. All this Jeet notices from behind walls and doors, his ears permanently tuned in her direction no matter where in the house she is. Her curiosity astounds him. Her daring. When she held his back like that he felt such an immense surge of love, for her and from her. He shakes his head, marvelling at his luck, that she loves him too, loves being close to him, as close as anyone could ever be.

'They won't feed on air, if that's what you're waiting for.'

Mai. How long had she been watching him, in this house where everyone is watched by someone?

'You were gawping at the china room,' she says.

'Was I?' He kneels to untie the bundle of grass fodder and starts spreading it into the trough. When the buffalo nose forward, he halts them with a 'Hup!' until the burlap sack is shaken empty and he rises back on to his feet. He can still feel his mother's stare, a weight against his cheek, and now she steps forward and runs a hand through his hair, tugging at it, tugging hard, until she relaxes her grip and lets her hand slide, her fingers weaving down the buttons on his chest. Jeet moves a little away.

'Dearest child, what if she doesn't give us a son? Think how glum you'll be if we have to set her aside for another. Let's not get too attached. Agreed?'

'What does it—'

She puts a finger to his mouth, presses, and runs the pad of her finger all along the inside of his bottom lip, up against his teeth. 'No more.' Then, relinquishing him: 'Such a pretty one. You did the right thing. Though I wouldn't have thought you'd have had it in you. Cheating your brother like that.'

'I have work.'

'Oh, don't feel so guilty. I called you Jeet for a reason. Of course you were going to win. Anyway,' she goes on, looking off towards the silent room, 'his is pretty, too, don't you think? With all her powders and mascara. I bet she's lots of jumpy fun.'

12

Finally, Mehar can hold it in no longer and she shows her sisters-in-law the pearls, one afternoon while they're preparing the evening meal.

'To help you have a boy?' Harbans asks.

Mehar nods. 'By the third crop. So the priest says.'

'So where are our pearls?' says Gurleen.

'Maybe Mai likes me best,' suggests Mehar.

'Or maybe you need the most help,' counters Gurleen, her voice delicately cruel.

'But look how beautiful they are,' says Harbans. 'I can see my face in them.' Then, a little wickedly: 'Did it make any difference?'

She doesn't know if it was the pearls, or the simple fact of carrying his face in her mind, but there was certainly a difference. She felt it ... down below. But how to say—

'It did!' Harbans exclaims. 'Look at your face!'

Mehar laughs, feeling herself getting carried away, *wanting* that feeling of getting carried away. 'Those trains we hear about? He was like one of those!'

'Common cows,' Gurleen says, but the other two can't stop laughing, and only do so when Mehar freezes and raises her head as if sniffing the air. Something is happening outside.

'You're the rotten fruit of his rotten seed.'

Calmly, Mai whacks the sugarcane across Suraj's calves, sending him buckling and reaching for the floor. She thrashes him again across the narrow width of his bare back, and then again, and again, until finally Suraj gives in, collapses on to his chest, and cries out.

Jeet comes running into the yard followed by the middle brother, Mohan. 'What are you doing!' Jeet bellows, snatching the cane away.

'Sold two of our herd and gambled away the money,' Mai says, laughing, though the laughter contains anger, even menace. The voicing of the crime reignites the rage and she takes back the cane and slams it into Suraj's head. This time it is Mohan who frees the stick from her hand and casts it aside.

'Enough,' Mai says, as if she was the peacemaker in all this, and Jeet drops to his knees and cradles his brother's head.

'Fetch the honey,' he says to Mohan, but Suraj pushes his examining hands away. He rises to his knees, glowering at his mother, who is looking down at him, imperious even in the way she tidies back her hair.

Mehar lets go of the window slat and darkness returns. Her eyes are wet. Perhaps she sniffles because Gurleen asks, 'Is he yours, do you wonder? The one on the floor?'

Yes, he is, she thinks. In a world where there is no word for privacy (not that she knows this), keeping this fact to herself is a way of silently claiming solidarity with her injured husband. 'I wouldn't know,' she tells Gurleen.

He doesn't request Mehar's company that night, or the night after that. She lies there in the dark, Harbans snoring unhurriedly at her side. The memory of him splayed across the ground, refusing to scream out, torments her. If he was with her, would she throw aside all caution and kiss his wounds, touch them with her lips? She feels certain that she would and out of this conviction flows liquid heat into her thighs. To keep the sensation from rising she brings her knees to her chest. Harbans protests sleepily. Mehar closes her eyes. Remembers the warmth of his body pressing against her. Her hand goes to her stomach, under her tunic, and fingers the drawstring of her salwar. It goes further, down to her hair. She sighs a shivery lusty sigh and opens her eyes, glancing around in the dark to check that no one has seen.

13

Bright afternoon, and Mehar sits on the edge of the stone bath snapping off the remaining wicker spokes and folding them into the latticework. She admires her finished basket, jumping it around in her hands, and then returns to the china room, where Harbans is cutting up fruit. She doesn't appear to have heard Mehar enter.

'Everything okay, sister?'

'Oh, sorry,' says Harbans, raising her head. 'That looks plenty big enough,' she adds, as Mehar drops the basket to the counter and begins lining it with squares of brown jute. Then, as if she'd been thinking on it for a while now: 'My sister said jute comes all the way from the east. It takes days to get here.'

'You've never mentioned your sister.'

Harbans shrugs, as if to say, what was the point? 'I think it's her wedding today.'

'As in – today?' Mehar looks appalled. 'Why in the name of Lord Krishna aren't you there? You should be there!'

Harbans turns away and starts on the next batch of fruit. Mai has ordered them to distribute it among the workers in the field.

'Did Mai stop you? The old witch.'

'It's for the best. Imagine how much my parents would have to wait on Mai, all the gold they'd have to send me back here with.' She brings the knife down hard.

Holding Harbans from behind, Mehar kisses her shoulder, though the embrace is as much for herself and her own sadness at not seeing Monty in so long. What would he be doing right now? Press-ups in the village square? Hectoring the locals who don't send their kids to school? She fears he is drifting away from her, and so, to touch something he has held, she darts into Mai's room and returns with the jamawar wedding shawl.

'Lord, that's beautiful,' Harbans says, wiping her hands down her front. Softly, she strokes its border, the woven intricacy of it all. 'Oh, my.'

'My brother helped me choose it. Tell you what, if she stops me from going to his wedding, I'll hide a scorpion in her salwar.'

'Poor scorpion!' Harbans says, and they laugh.

The shawl put back, the fruit cut, Harbans reaches for her veil and balances the basket on her head, all set to share it out.

'I'll do that,' Mehar says.

'No, no. Someone still needs to collect the dung.'

'I knew you'd give me that.'

Harbans grins, drops her veil.

'Where's Gurleen?' asks Mehar.

'At the temple. With Mai, don't you know?'

Mehar pulls herself up straight, as tall as Gurleen, and pitches her voice just so. 'Don't you think that even Mai's farts smell of attar of roses?'

'It's like she's in the room,' Harbans grins. 'Can you believe she refused to bring in the spinach? Said we can do it. I'll make her, you watch. Anyway' – she opens the door – 'don't forget.'

'Dung dung,' they say, in unison.

She naps first and by the time she wakes the house's shadow hangs across the yard. Another afternoon is dwindling. Crickets scrape in the branches. The first carts are wheeling out of the fields. Noises, noises. She walks quickly on her toes through the barn, closing her nose to the animal smells and exhaling only once she is out and standing by the buffalo enclosure at the rear of the house. Against the back wall the dung patties are heaped in a pyramid twice her height. She checks that the bulls are all tied up, then steps on to the brown field, anklets chiming as she scouts around for the big stick. She finds it lodged in the wheel of a wooden cart, heavy with fodder, and drags the stick to the pyramid of dung. Stretching up, straining, the sun on her face, she jabs the stick towards the topmost patty. She jumps, but still the stick won't reach and the thing won't fall. Muttering, she rolls her salwar bottoms up a few inches, begins scaling the ladder of bricks protruding from the wall and, agile as she is, is over halfway up when:

'Shall I get them?'

It doesn't cause her to slip, hearing a male voice. If anything it only strengthens her grip, as if that allows her to keep hold of her dignity. She turns her face away from his voice and into the meat of her elbow. She imagines Mai slapping her for flaunting her face like this. And her calves. Dear Lord, her bare calves. She tries jiggling her legs and, mercifully, the material drops silkily to her feet.

'You might fall. Let me do it.'

She starts to descend, and before both feet are back on the ground she grabs her veil and lurches it down her face. Her heart feels monumental in her chest. She steps aside to give him access to the brick-ladder but he doesn't need it and nimbly zigzags up the wall, his arm a lever he uses to swing himself high. At the top, like some prince straddling his horse, he kicks down one, two, three patties. She hears them land.

'More?'

'If it's no trouble,' she says.

'Well, how many then, if you would be so merciful?' *If you would be so merciful. Mehar-bani kar ke.*

Is he teasing her? Could it be him? Sickening joy leaps in her stomach.

'Come on,' he says gently.

'Only two more, please,' and the patties come thudding down by her feet and then his own feet land beside them. Next, in a moment that terrifies her, he crouches down to gather them up and suddenly his face is there and it is him, her husband, come to help her, and she feels her terror convert into delight. She wonders how long he had been watching her from the barn door before coming to her aid. She imagines him leaning into the doorframe, arms across his chest, chewing a bit of straw, watching her movements. The thought is intensely pleasurable. He stands and once more she can only see his feet.

'Where do you want them?'

And because it is her husband, and because they are alone, she lifts the veil clean off her face and folds it over the crown of her head. Her eyes feel huge to her, as if they take up more than half of her face. She looks at him and she could not be clearer, she could not be more wanton, he thinks, and his chest pumps so quickly it's obvious he's read her correctly. A long electric moment charges and forks about them. She wonders what he might be thinking. All she wants him to say is that he'll come to her tonight. Maybe she should ask him straight out? Why not, now she's gone this far already? He motions with his chin for her to follow him and he leads her back towards the barn, where the sun fills the doorway but intrudes no further. He puts down the patties and then moves, diagonally, to the corner of the room where the recess seems darkest. She doesn't know what he expects of her right now, standing in the middle of the barn. To collect the patties and go? She hopes he's not ashamed of her, of her unbecoming behaviour. She hopes she has not disgusted him. She tells herself that she's willing to argue her case, that she's not done anything unforgivably wrong. But even as she prepares herself, the question fades, and none of that seems to matter now because he's neither speaking to nor looking at her: he's clearing the ground. Nerves press her throat, forcing some words to pop out.

'How is your head now?' she asks.

'Hmm? Oh, you saw.'

She can tell he's embarrassed that she saw his beating. She shouldn't have mentioned it, but now that she has: 'It's not my place to criticise your mother, and perhaps I speak beyond my allowance, but I felt it was very cruel.'

He nods, still crouching. The cool whites of his eyes are large in the gloom. 'How long before everyone's back?'

'Until evening prayers, or maybe the first stars. They've still got to go to Kalyan's field for gourds. For the saag.' See? her look seems to say. I know things, too.

He holds out his arm, his palm cupped at the end of it, beckoning. She moves, anklet bells sounding, warning, and holding her wrist he pulls her down so she's crouching too. He lifts her tunic off her body, inside-outing it over her head. She shudders, her breasts open to the air and the breeze, nipples puckering. She can't object even if she wants to. He is her husband and he takes off his own tunic too and as he presses towards her she closes her arms around his neck and feels herself leaning into the ground.

How long had Suraj been watching Mehar? Long enough for the sun to move one whole degree along its path. For the grass to lengthen by the thickness of a fingernail. For the flock of starlings to abruptly pivot and zoom over the horizon, as if witnessing an event that had to be reported at once. He watched her. It was the first time he'd seen her, and he watched her. She was wrong about the crossed arms and piece of straw, and even about the lean into the doorway. He crouched as he watched, inside the entrance, his expression lost in shadow, his bare feet flat on the uneven ground. So this was his eldest brother's wife, the venerated sister-in-law, the one to whom, in time, once she'd delivered a son, he'd have to show the deepest respect and courtesy. Revere her as a second mother. The one who could then ask him, as her youngest brother-in-law, to do whatever she wanted, whatever task. A small kittenish smile comes to his lips. She's so much younger than him. And yet she is to be Mai's successor! To hold that exalted office! It all makes sense to him now, looking at the sinewy bare calves, the wide lush mouth pursed in climbing concentration. The huge eyes. Her bright skin. The confusion hadn't been a confusion at all. He had been right all along. His brother had changed his mind.

Suraj had been playing his dhol for all of that afternoon when Mai and Jeet went visiting the brides, jamming and

97

practising, trying to mimic the drummers he'd applauded and whistled during the parades the previous week. How fine they'd looked, in their azure tunics and peacock hats. How *modern*. And how eagerly the women had crowded the balconies to admire the young musicians. He was determined to be part of the parade the following year, if only his damned left hand would do as it was told. It kept falling in rhythm with his right, when he needed it to drum a three-quarter beat, a syncopation that filled the gaps. Still, he had seemed to be getting somewhere when he heard his brother and Mai return on the bullock cart. He carried on, adjusting the strap around his sweaty neck so the drum rested at an angle across his torso, ignoring their calls for him to come out into the yard. Finally, Jeet entered the room and asked him to please come, that Mai was waiting. Mohan was already there, wet and grubby from hosing down the animals, his hands bent back on his hips.

'You could have given your brother a hand,' Jeet suggested, as Suraj joined them without quite joining them, standing outside of their triangle and with his dhol still hanging off his neck.

'Done nothing but play that flaming drum all afternoon,' Mohan said. His eyes were bloodshot. He liked meeting the village drunks of an evening, Mohan did, but this vice was forgiven because he was also the hardest of workers. No matter the heat, he could be seen out there in the field, the alcohol sweating out of him.

'The weddings are next month,' Mai said. 'We need all hands for the tilling, so after that. Maybe the seventeenth. It depends how the crops are looking.'

'And their families are happy with that?' Mohan asked.

'They'll do whatever they're told. But go to the temple tomorrow. And be sure to tell the priest we're keeping it small. No need for a big song and dance.'

'Shame,' Mohan said, cuffing Suraj's ear. 'You could have played your drum.'

'We'll do it all on the same day,' Mai went on. 'Their villages are close enough.'

'It'll be cheaper,' Jeet explained.

'And we won't have to be away from home so much,' Mohan reasoned.

'Good,' Mai said. 'I'll order some foreign cloth while we can. That Vijaypal near the corner stand seems to think he can still get some. And have that floor marbled, will you?'

'The whole floor?' asked Mohan, puffing out his cheeks. Another job for him.

'The inside bit only. Don't waste it outside their room.'

'If you have to play your dhol, you'll need to find somewhere else,' Jeet said. 'Like Mai says, that room's theirs.'

Suraj said nothing. He had no interest in getting married. There were no happy husbands as far as he could see. Or wives, for that matter. He only hoped she'd leave him alone, whoever she was. Even sex was no longer an enticing prospect, not now he'd acquainted himself with the city brothels. He scratched the back of his neck with the end of his drumstick – the strap was chafing again.

'How old are they?' Mohan asked. 'Can they handle cattle?'

'They better,' replied Mai. 'They say yours is seventeen. Yours too,' she added, looking at Suraj.

He popped his tongue against the inside of his cheek. 'She's aged quick. Last week you said she was barely of age.'

'She's seventeen. No arguments.'

'And yours, brother?' he asked Jeet.

Jeet's mouth twitched. Even as a child, swapping plates so he got the bigger dollops of butter, he could never hide his guilt and would be forced to swap them back. 'I'm not sure. They said fourteen-fifteen.'

'And you in your twenty-third year. For shame.'

'It's decided,' Mai said. 'The priest, he's been given the pairings.'

Suraj gave her a sour smile. 'Are we to understand that he saw all three and persuaded you to change your mind?'

'You're getting things mixed up,' Mai said.

'You don't even care, do you? That he's cheating me out of what's mine. Why would you.'

She slapped him, hard, though his head barely moved. 'I said, you're confused.'

And he said nothing more, not in the days to come, nor after the wedding, because he supposed she was right: that a wife was a wife, there to bear sons and otherwise live behind her veil, out of his way. Her face was barely worth considering.

Now, he crushes her underneath him, sucking at her breasts and thrusting so insistently the crown of her head jerks closer and closer to the wall. It is an assault. Her face no longer registers in his mind. He feels desire, yes, but it is also about pain and revenge and what he believes to be rightfully his. And, after all, this is no more than such an immodest woman deserves.

When it is over, he expects her to clutch her clothes to her chest and sprint off in tears, is waiting for it. But she is not crying. She is using both arms to reach behind her back and twist together the tiny metal clasps of her tunic. Astonishingly, she doesn't seem to be in the slightest hurry. She pulls her long hair over one shoulder, running her fingers through the black screen of it all. He tries to muster up some hatred for this casual woman: there is not even a passing look of shame on her face. How lucky, in fact, that he avoided marrying her. Even the red-lipped courtesans have the grace to appear wounded once he's finished with them. At this thought the hatred comes swiftly but it is complicated and eclipsed by a twenty-year-old's sense of wonder. Her smile is so calm, her face so eloquent. She stands, smoothing down the back of her tunic, and lifts both hands to draw her hair away from her face and coil it into a knot at the back of her head. Her arms rest at her sides.

'May I speak?' she asks.

'No.'

She frowns, making a funny little face at him, then palms up her anklets, draws her veil forward and turns to go. Her silk-dark hips oscillate through the gloom. He finds he wants her to stay, a feeling that has as much to do with her body, with both of their bodies, with the playful cast of her face, as it does with the unacknowledged desire he carries inside him to destroy this world. Above the barn, fireflies gather in blooms of yellow. Will he let her simply walk away?

'I want to meet you again.'

She pauses at the barn entrance, her back to him, and lowering her heel to the ground she turns her head to one side. 'You mean tonight, my lord?'

Lord! What a mind. Can fell him with a word. He can feel the need rising in him, as it clearly still does in her. She is so quietly sensual, so serenely ravenous. He wriggles up and off his elbows, sitting cross-legged, suddenly a student before her. A thin layer of dust covers the outside of his bare thighs. 'I'd love to meet you tonight.'

'You'll need to tell Mai, then.'

He smiles. How different she is. 'Maybe I will,' he replies, and she steps out of the empty doorway and into the courtyard. The stars, already out, are confusing, and she panics that it is later than she thought and what if the women have returned and witnessed or heard her and her husband? But they are not in the room and some time passes before she hears Harbans asking Gurleen to fetch the widest of the giant trays, the paraats, and to get a shuffle on because all this gourd and saag she has on her head is beginning to make her dizzy. Mehar comes out to lend a hand and together they transfer the green pickings, spreading the velvety leaves and wiping them of any dirt.

'It got dark quickly,' Gurleen says.

'Hmm,' yawns Harbans, pausing to drag a tired forearm across her brow. Then: 'Well, will you look at that.'

The other two turn. A shimmering column dancing across the roof of the barn.

'Fireflies?' Gurleen says. 'What a strange night. Maybe the monsoon is coming early.'

Mehar is still staring: they look so bright and magical. She wonders if he is still in the barn and thinking of her, as she is of him.

Long after he hears the women repair to their room, Suraj stays in the barn, sitting up against the mud wall. He knows he should clean away the discs of shit around the buffalo, that his brothers will berate him when they return, but all he wants to do is sit here in the kindly dark and think of her. Her huge clever eyes and satin skin. The gentle arcs of her eyebrows. A hand-span waist he could not stop himself from biting until he went lower and looked up and saw her mouth quivering and wet. Her hands had squeezed his back and the electricity of that moment has not left him. Next time, he will not be rough. Was he too rough? No matter. Next time, he will be as gentle as the hollows at the base of her throat. When he hears his mother return, and then his brothers, Suraj takes up his wrap, shakes it free of dirt, and arranges it into a small tight turban. He doesn't want them to see his hair, which is to say he doesn't want them to see that he has cut his hair, the first in his family ever to do so. That it now only falls as far as his shoulders. The previous week he'd gone to the Mohammedan barber in the bazaar and handed over a rupee and a warning to keep his mouth shut.

Suraj rises to his feet and it is this, the mechanics of standing up, that cause the first domino to fall, a chain of synaptic flares deep in the bowl of his brain. Him taking off her top. The smile. Her calm. My lord. Tell Mai. Tell Mai? Before he's even at the doorway his tread has slowed to a standstill. He reaches for the wall. Forces himself to think. And as his fingers close into a fist, he sees what has happened, and quietly crouches to the ground and puts his face in his hands.

14

She won't say anything. She can't. Her own obliteration would result. Her head shaved and her naked body paraded through the village on the end of a rope. She would be made into an example. Or, if not that, if Mai decided to show mercy and not throw her out, then at the very least her status in the household would be no more. No more the respected wife of the eldest brother. Everyone's bhabhi. She would live at the bottom of the pile. Constant insinuations from the sisters-in-law. Sly put-downs from Mai. No right of reply. And, inevitably, the story would leak out to the village and into people's homes. These things always do. Whenever she ventured into the bazaar for some small thing – a handful of okra, a dozen eggs – it would be there, the opprobrium following her every turn. Not letting her ever rest, not lending her mind any peace at all, but suffocating her, the small village and their small minds tormenting her until she slinks back to the farm and has to face it all again, for ever, until she dies and even then it will become a thing spoken about, a legend passed on, the story of the daughter-in-law who ensnared the brothers of her husband, the courtesan, the Phryne, so that she'd be denied even the solace of death, consigned to bare her teeth and claw the inside of her coffin as she burned in judgement.

'Are you eating your roti or strangling it?'

Suraj looks down to his food, his grip already loosening. 'Sorry,' he says inaudibly. It is evening again, a whole day since he caught her climbing the wall, poking at the patties with her stick.

'Getting dark earlier this month,' Mai goes on. 'The moon's enormous again.'

'Flaunting herself,' Jeet says, and Suraj pauses with the food at his lips, then he closes his mouth around the roti and chews so slowly he can feel each click of his jaw. Does Jeet know? Has she, in her great innocence, let it all slip through her hands? He allows the thought to bat around his mind as he takes in another mouthful. No one would say a word to him. Not even his brother. Mai would make sure of that. For the sake of the family, for the glory of the family, she'd ensure that the shame rained down on her errant daughter-in-law only. And there is that image again: her in the market while the vendor smirks on. *Can I get a night with you as well, sister?* Her tears burning as she leaves the coins on the wood-wormed counter and takes the small string bag with its brown eggs.

'Uff, pass it here if you're just going to stare at it,' Mai says. 'A half-decent roti going to waste.'

'Will you help me clear the shit from the barn,' Jeet asks, and Suraj nods and claps his hands clean. The door to their room opens up ahead and one of the women steps out with a brass pot of water. They must have been watching through the slatted window – *she* must have been watching – waiting to see when the water should be brought out. It is not her, though, he realises, with a strange relief that also feels like disappointment. No, it is his own wife. She places before him a steel bowl containing a gnarled stump of pale grey soap and when he takes the soap and holds his hands out, she tips the brass pot and pours. He washes restlessly, his hands, his mouth, his beard, snatching at the stiff towel she offers and scrubbing his nails free of turmeric, and then he stands as if he has something urgent he must attend to, looking around, at anywhere but at his wife. Is *she* watching him from behind the slats still? Are the women the ones who can see everything, while the men stare at black windows? He steps away to the barn, three ravines inscribed across his forehead.

'Where are you going?' asks Mai.

'To clear the shit,' he says.

'So why waste soap washing your hands?'

15

The sun rises and sets, rises and sets, and in the long intervening hours Suraj keeps himself away: joining friends in the bazaar to marvel sceptically at a new thing called a wireless radio; on his drum near the tannery; dozing in the shade while cattle slurp at the reedy swamp. He leaves home via the barn and crosses the field at a time when he knows she will be out collecting patties, and he doesn't return until moon-up, once she is safely in her room alongside her sisters. By that time, the gates are locked, so he takes a running jump, heaves himself up on to the sandstone wall and leaps over the stone bath. He stands in the empty courtyard: above him, the stars are bright and stitched into the day's dark dress. They are so close he could reach up to twist away a sequin and when he does run his palm across the night, the stars travel along his arm. He wonders what lies beyond them.

God, he supposes, with his set of brass scales. Suraj doesn't move when he hears … what? Slippers. A cough. Not a minute later: a door. His eldest brother emerges from the room the men share and crosses to the water pump by the barn. He looks small as he works the lever with one hand, drinking from the other, bent over like a nocturnal animal taking its surreptitious chance. He finishes by splashing his face, and when he stands his bony nub of a shoulder jerks up slightly, as if it may be hurting him a little. Suraj feels something like affection, and for half a moment there is equilibrium in this velvet hour, his love for his brother balanced silently and perfectly with his desire for his brother's wife. A snake side-winds along the sandy wall and as Suraj watches its tail vanish under the metal gate, Jeet starts his move across the courtyard and at once a giant weight crashes through Suraj. All he knows is that he must stop him.

'Brother,' he says, stepping into the moonlight.

Jeet doesn't start and Suraj wonders if for all this time his brother has been alert to his presence. 'What is it?'

'One of the Bawa boys said they saw a Mussulman at our well earlier. At Murnalipur.'

Jeet turns, facing Suraj square on. 'And what did you find there?' he asks, though the question is inflected with sarcasm. Not for the first time Suraj wonders if his brother hates him on some level, hates him for not having to be the eldest male in the house and for all that comes with it.

'I've not been. I thought I'd tell you. Do you think someone's messing with the irrigation again?'

'Go, can't you?'

Suraj smiles, very deliberately. 'Why can't you go?'

There's a controlled look of difficulty on Jeet's face, a sharpening of his triangular jawline. 'Don't be a child. Now go.' He starts to walk away, towards the back chamber.

'Got what you want, didn't you?' Suraj blurts. 'Mother and son sewed it up so it all worked out nicely. For you.'

Jeet turns but doesn't meet his eyes. 'I don't know what you mean.'

'What does she look like, anyway?'

'That's no way for you to speak about her.'

'That was no way for a brother to behave.'

Jeet groans angrily, then steps to the gate, where the cumbersome process of unlocking it sounds obscenely loud at this hour.

'The swamp flooded so maybe go via the lower market,' Suraj advises, as Jeet takes the bicycle from where it rests against the wall and rides shakily off.

One hundred. Two hundred. Three hundred, he counts, barely working his lips and standing unmoving in the yard, in the moon. The sun in the moon. He looks about him, from the quiet of the barn to the charpoys stowed upright under the veranda, their long round legs like rifles, all the way across to the china room, shuttered in silence. He'd skipped over the double-doors at the rear of the porch. Now, he walks towards them, applies his hand to the flaking paint and steals inside, to where Mehar has been instructed to wait for her husband.

She is careful not to display her joy when, for a change, he doesn't sit up and leave in the moments after he has finished. Instead, he lies there, and she imagines his nape snug against the tubular cushion, his eyes open and fixed to the ceiling. Sorrowful eyes, she remembers. He has one hand in his hair and the bony point of his elbow is right by her forehead, not quite touching. She convinces herself she can see it.

'*Mujhe tumse kuch baat karni hai.*' I'd like to have a word with you. And so formal!

She feels her eyes widen. She smiles. 'I'd be honoured.'

There's a shifting in the darkness as he turns on to his side, towards her. She waits, eyes lowered, her wrist starting to ache under her cheek. When he finds and touches her face, by her chin, lightly, tenderly, with just one finger, in a way she never thought her husband would ever touch her, she feels her lips part and hears her own breath, warm and thick. She wonders if he can hear it too, and he thinks that he can, and then he is sure of it, of the feel of it on his wrist as he strokes her face, her eyes, the skin around her nose-gem, opening up his hand to take in the full sweep of her beautiful lambent cheek. He trails his thumb down her arms, releasing her hand from under her face and kissing her palm, licking it. He can feel the rush in his blood, the clamour and the desire, and knows he can't say anything now. The baat, the word, will have to wait. And he is gorging on her brown-tipped nipples and her hands are tugging at the loose turban of his hair and their ache for each other is like a real thing that can be touched and smelled and, it must surely be said, heard.

16

The sun lances in through the slats and Mehar leans her hip on the stone slab of the counter, her face held in the heel of one hand and her elbow cupped in the other. She looks asleep, and she might be, or might have been, but she seems aware of Gurleen's fidgety intemperance. The kettle is put down too hard. The carrots sliced too deliberately. Dreamily, Mehar pushes her mind past all this and to the sound of the teacher humming on his way home. She must have seen him before, walking the track behind their room, because she is sure of his large stomach, of his spectacles and blue turban and scruffy beard, the brown satchel of exercise books hooked over his shoulder. She listens to his lovely humming until she can no longer even imagine that she can hear it. She opens her eyes. Gurleen hauls a large rattan basket up on to the counter and impales one of the aubergines with her knife.

Mehar, swallowing a smile, makes a start on the evening dough.

After the men have been fed, she collects the last of the dishes from the courtyard, and though behind the house the sun is sinking, under her veil everything is light-filled, the air full of that exquisite sense of a long day falling towards its end. Inside the china room, Gurleen is squatting on the floor, running the dirty plates through a tub of sudsy water.

'Some more, sister,' Mehar says, adding to the pile.

Gurleen, her face set hard, slaps down the wet rag and leaves, claiming she left some chillies on the roof.

Mehar takes over at the tap. 'Is she okay? All day she's been cross.'

Saying nothing, Harbans brings a cleaver down on a frantic mouse that's been ravaging their grain. She winces as the warm blood spurts, then, lowering her veil, she foots open the door and casts the two grungy pieces into the field. She hears them land in the reedy grass, sees a kestrel already circling overhead, then lets the door swing shut, nudging Mehar aside to wash the stringy blood from her hands.

'Can't you do that at the pump?' Mehar says, annoyed.

'Her husband. He's not been asking for her,' Harbans says, in a measured tone, as if choosing her words carefully. 'She's worried.'

Mehar offers her a cloth to dry her hands. 'You know, I thought it might be something like that. Poor thing. They never think of us.'

'Were you visited last night?' Harbans asks, accepting a bowl that needs putting away. 'By your husband?'

'Hmm? Yes. Why?'

'No reason. It's nothing. You know what a fool Gurleen can be. But last night she overheard two of the men talking.'

'About what?'

'I don't know. Then one of them cycled away.'

'They come and go as they please. Barely a care to their name.'

Mehar hands across the last plate, but when she stands she sees that there are tears on Harbans' cheeks.

'What's this?'

'Nothing. I feel for her, is all.' She pulls Mehar close, and holds her as though she fears never seeing her again. 'I'm sure it'll sort itself out.'

17

By then, in the high summer of 1929, there was talk throughout the state that revolutionaries were going from village to village, farm to farm, taking by force valuables that weren't offered willingly. Some said to give to those made destitute by British foreign policy. Others to fund the purchase of ammunition for the Free India movement. Either way, Mai decided she'd better make her annual pilgrimage to Amritsar while she could, before men on camels blocked the roads and things got too dicey to travel. She would take Jeet and be away for six days.

On each of these nights Mehar steals away to the fields, where the wheat is now tall, where Suraj waits. It is his idea that they leave the farm and meet underneath the stars.

One night, she brings the pearls and holds them high against the black sky, as if placing a garland around the moon. How small it all is, she thinks. What a brocade we make of life.

'Why fetch them?' Suraj asks.

'I don't know. Maybe I've got used to them. You got them for me.'

He releases her from his hold and rolls on to his back. 'Mumbo-jumbo rubbish. Put them away.'

She lies there quietly, defying him, watching the patterns above. Then she shakes her salwar and slides it back on.

'Don't go,' he says.

'Oh, I think I will.' It is their third night in a row like this and she knows she can get away with saying all sorts of things now. Knows also that she enjoys some control over her husband.

'Once more?' he says.

She laughs. 'Tomorrow.'

'Tomorrow,' he repeats, sighing.

'We're lucky we can be together.' She wants to say something more. She wants to share something of her own world with him, to draw him closer into her ordinary concerns. 'Not everyone is blessed. My poor sister – she is so upset.'

'Upset?' he says, turning his face away.

'It's Gurleen.' She wonders whether to carry on – might he think her trivial, in some way? – and then she does: 'Your brother hasn't wanted her company for many days now. Perhaps he's going elsewhere. To the city.'

Suraj nods. The dark. The bats snapping through the dark. The whole wide and dark world.

'She may well speak to Mai as soon as she's back.'

Let that day not come, he thinks. Asks: 'And when is she back?'

He says 'she' with such heavy distaste it makes Mehar smile. He can be such an old woman sometimes. 'Two-three days? Is it six temples she's visiting?'

'God knows.'

'I guess He'll be hearing her prayers for grandsons.' Then: 'I hope children come but not too soon. Don't you?'

He doesn't know. Doesn't want to speak or think about anything any more. Wants only to enjoy these next few days with her and then he'll confess. Somehow, somehow.

'Which of your brothers is hers?' She feels able to ask this extraordinary question now. He won't mind. He knows the question conceals nothing sinister about her wifely character. But mind he does:

'What business is it of yours to think about other men?'

He speaks with such anger that it ignites a flame of injustice inside her. She stands and he flips to his knees, reaches for her wrist and coaxes her back down. He hasn't expected to have poured so much of himself into her hands.

'So tomorrow?' he asks again.

Her front teeth rest on her lower lip and moonlight breaks over the parting in her hair. Even her ears are beautiful. How can ears be beautiful? She was made for him, for him to own, of this he is certain, and certain too that he would trample over his own grave to possess her.

'I'd like that,' she says and the simplicity of her words, the way they connect to the honesty of her face, rouses a shame that stokes his desire and forces his heart to augment, as if it were making room for a new kind of emotion.

She doesn't veil her face and they talk in a low, laughing undertone all the way home, until Suraj hangs back behind the gate and she continues through.

'Sisters!' Mehar whispers, slipping inside the china room. 'You asleep?'

'Just get in,' Harbans replies, and Mehar lowers herself on to the charpoy, checking that the noisy anklet bells she'd taken off are still there, under the pillow.

18

There was a moment when Mehar had been about to tell Harbans that the brother sitting on the chair was her husband. But before she could get the words out, Harbans covered her ears, saying she didn't want to know, didn't need to know.

'So you know which is yours?' Mehar asked.

'Please. Stop. It'll all be fine. It'll all be fine.' Mehar nodded, turned back to the slatted window, perplexed. She assumed Harbans must be having marital difficulties, but when she tried to talk to Gurleen about this, she too turned immediately away.

'Don't talk to me about the men,' she said, blustering off with an armful of kindling. Mehar, shaking her head, followed with the patties and together they got the mud-oven going, for Mai was returning from her pilgrimage and everything had to be made fresh.

'But are you going to speak to her about your husband?' Mehar asks, tentatively, and when Gurleen doesn't reply, Mehar touches her arm and tells her not to worry.

That evening, once Mai arrives with Jeet and her younger sons have touched her feet and everyone is fed and out of the yard, Gurleen approaches her mother-in-law, asking for a word alone. Mehar watches from the window as Mai reluctantly rises from her charpoy and leads Gurleen into her room. Left with the empty courtyard, where the moon on the ground glimmers brokenly, like a shoal of ghostly fish, Mehar feels confusion pulling her under. She never thought Gurleen, or Harbans, or any of them, would be brave enough, brazen enough, to criticise Mai's son directly to Mai's face. That Gurleen is doing exactly this unnerves her, as if the rules of the cosmos are being challenged. When Gurleen returns, Mehar asks, 'How did she take it? Will she tell him to treat you better?' But once again she doesn't respond. There has undoubtedly been something strange in her sisters' behaviour of late. A certain atmosphere in the room, an exchange of freighted glances. Mehar explains away these moments – distant husbands, the struggles of conception – and almost wills herself to leave the matter be.

It is long past midnight when Mehar is woken by what sounds like anger, and when she rises to the window and pushes down the slat, she sees one of the brothers emerge from Mai's room and stand in the porch, hitting the wall again and again. Ah, Gurleen's husband, Mehar thinks unsympathetically. He must have got a lashing from his mother.

19

Suraj had not confessed to Mehar, the night before Mai's return. As Mehar shook the crud from her slippers and stood to leave, he had stood up too, full of a sudden energy he didn't know how to dispense. She'd looked surprised.

'You're like a bag of weasels.'

'It's nothing. I'm just thinking.' On some level, he seemed to realise that if he were to confess now it would be the end of it, her trauma and rage would ensure that nothing salvageable could remain; but if she found out in the house, surrounded by the rest of the family, she'd have to submerge her anger and perhaps, in its stead, whatever grew might be more likely to bend towards him. 'When will I have you again?' he asked despairingly.

She smiled, a look of puzzlement that seemed almost maternal in its affection. 'Back to normal.'

He nodded and didn't say much on the walk home. Yes, better that she works it out for herself, but better for whom, he doesn't dare wonder; he just waits. He lies on his charpoy at night and he waits, for as soon as she is told that her husband wants to spend the night with her it will all be over. He imagines her lying in the back room when Jeet enters. Will she know from his first touch, now she's become so familiar with his own? Will she push him away, demanding he get out at once? She will not shout; of that he is certain. She will not draw attention to this aspect of life. He prays she does not say anything that might reveal their secret, for her own sake. That thought he finds unbearable. So he lies there wide awake, night after night, in silent and dreadful anticipation, waiting to hear his brother rise from his charpoy, which is mere yards from Suraj's own, and cross the courtyard. Except that he doesn't. His brother only sleeps, his dark form curled away towards the wall. Twice Jeet did get up, on consecutive nights, and each time Suraj stared at the damp ceiling, his stomach a torrid knot as he swallowed with difficulty and refused to let the tears slide out of his eyes. But Jeet only ever went as far as the water pump, taking a drink before returning to their room, and as he lay back on his bed, Suraj could have hated him for not putting him out of this misery. So it is almost a relief when, one morning, Mai calls him from where she is fanning herself on her charpoy, enjoying the shade of the wide porch. In the barn, Suraj removes his dhol from around his neck and comes out into the yard.

'Me?'

'My pet,' she says, beckoning, and he crosses the dusty square, stopping a foot or so away. 'Sit. Sit with your old mother awhile.'

Warily, he does. She must want something. His head is lowered, his long fingers threaded loosely together to bridge the thin struts of his knees.

'Why is my boy so sad these days? Is that any way for a man of this family to behave?'

'Would you prefer it if I got drunk, gambled half our land away and then hanged myself?'

'You remind me of him in so many ways.'

'And you never miss a chance to tell me.'

'How angry!'

She is spinning the fan so fast, the flies at their feet seem to be playing in its breeze. They hover, then land across her toes. Hover. And land. Hover. And land. Her smile brings out the fine embroidery of her face, the delicate wrinkles glistening with sweat.

'You've got to go to the city and order me three salwar kameez. Make sure they're in the Patiala style. And saffron-khalsa colours. In case those thieving revolutionaries come. We want to look pious, no? You know Munim's store, in Anarkali?'

'What do I know about women's clothes? Stick your arse in a cart and go yourself.'

'Happily, if I could trust my daughters-in-law to manage things here,' she says, loud enough for them to hear in their room. 'A few days I was away and I'm still sorting out the mess. Who leaves flour out uncovered, I ask you, eh, who?' Then, back to her son: 'Off you go. The cart's free, take it.'

'Talk sense, woman.'

'You'll be back in time for roti.'

'I'm not doing your shopping!'

'My days! Normally fires in hell can't keep you from the city. Take your wife, then. Go on.'

There is a commotion in the china room, which soon dies down.

'Take what?' he says, the breath falling out of him.

'Why, your wife, child, who else? Take her. But don't pay him.' She points the fan at Suraj; the flies all land at once. 'The scoundrel will keep us waiting months otherwise.'

He stands and moves to the gate.

'Where are you going?'

'The cart.'

'Take your wife, I said. Even better, if she's with you, you can get one or two more things. For their room. Bowls and whatnot.' Then: 'There's no need to look like someone's shat in your shoe. I'll explain it all to her. Go fetch her, go on.'

'I'll be fine on my own. Quicker.'

'You won't know the stores. Just go and call her.'

'On my own. I'll be fine.' Heat prickles up his neck, horribly.

'Get her. She's probably waiting already. Ears like bats when they want to, those three.'

Suraj, relenting, face crumpling: 'Will you do it?'

'What is this nonsense, Suraj? Get her now.'

Inside the room, at the sound of him approaching, all three women reach for their heads and snap down their veils. Mehar smiles, eyes lowered, heart loud in her chest, and a new bride all over again. Riding into the city with her husband. The two of them, for all to admire. She imagines her sisters-in-law's faces when she returns in the evening. 'I've known for a while,' she will say. 'Isn't he the most handsome of them all?' Might she also tell them of all they did on their nights together, when Mai was away? No, no. That should remain a lovely secret, something forever untouched. When the sunlight on her knees is momentarily dimmed, she knows he must have passed across the slatted window, and seconds later she hears the door opening. His shadow – his legs, those narrow shoulders – lengthens over the grey stone floor, his head finishing somewhere by her sandalled feet. She is almost rising off the charpoy when he says: 'Might you please come with me, Gurleen?'

20

'Is everything all right?'

He blinks away the tears and rolls his shoulder to destroy those that have already spilled down his face. He thought he'd been silent but evidently not silent enough, for she's realised from behind her veil.

'I think Mai plotted this trip,' Gurleen goes on. 'For us to go together, I mean.'

'Because you spoke to her? Because I've not been asking for you?'

She says nothing.

'What does it matter,' he says, and he cracks the rein, once, twice, then again and harder again, determined to force the animal to circle towards the city gate and do as it is told.

21

Something in the way the moth flits at the slats, the way it gloats about the flimsy seeping light, brings on the sensation. It is as if the insect is deliberately exposing to Mehar its little hissing head, the bristling crawl of its legs. She hauls herself up, a hand to her sweat-glazed forehead, but she feels herself being pushed back down. There are voices, smudged sounds. Is it a man? God, no. Please no. Where's her veil? Is she veiled? She tries to scream, but all her energy seems taken with the effort to keep her breath, which is coming horribly short and fast. The doctor gives a few tugs to reset the mercury and then tries again with the thermometer. He asks one of the women to lift the patient's tunic so he might inject the quinine directly into her stomach. 'It'll dissolve better in her own acid,' he adds, smiling all round, feeling the need to explain why he is asking for the girl to be partially undressed in front of him, a Muslim. These Sikhs can be temperamental. Working in the fields – in this heat! – it must addle their brains. He rubs zinc lotion into Mehar's feet and leaves a phial of white oil on the stone counter with instructions to allow her a sip of it each morning. Finally, he presses borax into the lacerations she has made on her arms and neck, an application that causes the poor girl to thrash and wail before she succumbs to exhaustion and sleep once more.

22

This time, when Mehar wakes, it is dark, terrifyingly so. She needs air. She needs to throw up. Her head feels heavy and black, as if her neck were no stronger than a piece of straw. Reaching for her veil, she pushes up on to her feet, waits for the dizziness to settle, and then nego-tiates her way out of the room, across the courtyard, and to the edge of the wheat fields. She is not sick, though feels certain she needs to be, and the moon isn't helping, hanging so bewilderingly high. Nothing is helping. She takes some long breaths and slowly turns on her heel, keeping her head very still, and she's a few steps back into the yard when she sees his shadow and then him, sitting oddly against the wall, levitating. His eyes are as white as chalk. Has he been here the whole time? When did he return? Is she imagining this? She swallows, panic rising up her throat. Back in the room, she stares at the stone floor, at the gecko calmly eating its own leg. Or perhaps she is imagining that, too. Mehar closes her eyes.

'No better?' Harbans asks, an arm around her. 'Try to sleep. Get in with me.'

From the second charpoy, Gurleen huffs, and as Mehar falls on to her bed she sees in her mind's eye that it was his upended dhol, his drum, that he was sitting on, there against the wall.

***

Once we had smashed off the bolts and Laxman had planed the door, I took up residence. Mosquitoes rarely entered that room and at dusk the bats flew straight past with their tiny busy noise. A long stone slab stuck out from the wall and I kept my suitcase and rucksack open on that, along with my toothbrush, shower gel, bar of soap, and sixteen-pack of LuxGo toilet paper. I'd arranged my charpoy in the corner by the window, which I'd uncovered, prising a thick square of wood away from the ledge and then kicking it off. As the light streamed past the five iron bars and made a cage on the wall behind me, I wondered if Laxman had looked at me so hard because he saw a family resemblance. I'd always been told I take after my mother's side, it was true, and now I thought of my great-grandmother lying here, cooking here, in this small room with its forbidding bars.

At first the room reeked of stale smoke, of dung and overripe fruit, but washing the walls and leaving the door open got rid of the smell, or maybe I stopped noticing it, at least during the day. The only thing I couldn't scrub clean was a semicircle of ashy grime, signs of a cooking fire, about a foot wide and directly beneath the counter. At night, though, faint smells returned and what sleep I got was flooded by images of decaying fruit, of mulch and maggots. When that happened, I got up, climbed the stairs to the flat roof, breathed. Everything was black and quiet. I couldn't see the ground below me and had a sense of being free from gravity, of floating off into some corner of space. It reminded me of the first time I jacked up, and how I came home, went up to my room and stared out at the night. My vague reflection in the window was superimposed across the dark sky and, for once, looking at my face didn't feel difficult. It felt almost wonderful. I switched on my torch and cast a beam across the farm, over the barn. The moths came rapidly and I watched them swarm and flit in the wide cone of light.

One afternoon, a woman arrived on a green bicycle while I was poking a stick at a scorpling, prodding it into my bucket. It gibbered about, clawing at the iron sides, and I was at the water pump ready to drown the thing, when she told me not to. I did it anyway, threw scorpling and water high across the field and returned to the yard, where she was waiting, standing very straight with her bicycle at her side. She looked familiar, tall, graceful, but I couldn't place her. Her hair was uncombed and scrunched back, as if she'd tied it in a hurry, and she had the kind of face, with its strange semi-smile, that even in repose seemed wry.

'I was going to say you should burn it. They can survive a bit of water.'

She must be on her way to the next village, a couple of kilometres further down the track. Come to see how the foreigner was getting on, no doubt. She wasn't the first. There'd been several intrigued and uninvited visitors in those early days, locals who'd heard that the English grandson was living alone on the ragged farm. That Kuku had thrown him out. They never stayed long, and I was too wary to ask them to.

'Can I help you?'

'Your uncle asked me to give you this. Seeing as I was coming this way.'

Her bike had a front basket of thick white wire and she handed me an envelope lying flat at the bottom of it. My A level results. I'd given permission for my dad to collect the grades on my behalf, and he must have called Jai with the news. I slid the paper into my back pocket and frowned, the sun in my eyes. 'Thank you.'

'All good, I hope?'

'It's all fine. But I shouldn't take up any more of your time.'

I expected her to remount her bicycle and head out of the gate. Instead, she surprised me: she leaned her bike

135

against the wall, freed the hem of her long skirt from where it had snagged on a spoke and turned to the house, smiling at it.

'I've always wondered about this place, every time I come this way.'

She really was tall, our faces were almost level, and I was over six foot. 'Do you ride out here often?'

'Oh, not really.' She gave a small laugh. 'I made it sound as if I'm always racing by, didn't I? Once a fortnight, maybe. Whenever I'm setting up a drop-in at Sunra.'

She was the doctor, of course, the one who'd visited my uncle's house that time. Her name was Radhika, she told me, Radhika Chaturvedi, and now she was here she seemed intent on exploring. Leaving me at the pump, she ambled about the porch, a hand on one of the flaking pillars. 'Is it your family's?'

'It's my uncle's.'

'And is your uncle not your family?' She gave me a shrewd look and walked over to the barn, asking, 'What's through here?' but went inside before I could reply. When she returned to the yard I was in my room, rubbing sun cream into my face. It was in those minutes, with us both in separate parts of the house, that I realised she was different from others. 'Do you get many visitors?' she called.

'No welcome ones,' I said, stepping outside again.

She made a face, faux hurt. 'Going for the whole castaway look, I see. I don't remember a beard the last time we met.'

I crossed back to the pump, where a pile of my clothes were waiting to be washed, and bent down over the bucket.

'Can I ask you a question?'

I twisted around. Sunshine on her hair. Her face backlit.

'After you threw that scorpion away, as you came towards me, you rolled down your sleeves. Why?'

I hadn't realised I'd done that, it had become so much a reflex, but I said I thought she knew why and then neither of us spoke for the longest while. When I moved away, saying there was something upstairs I wanted to show her, she followed me up to the roof, and from there I gestured back across the fields, over the main centre of the village, to some red scaffolding erected around a stump the colour of blue sky.

'What are they building?'

'That statue thing? It's going to be Krishna, I think.'

'In the middle of nowhere?'

'In a field owned by some feudal lord or other. God knows these village ways. From what I hear he's having it built huge so it looks down over the village. Protectively.'

She took a red packet, some Marlboros, from a pocket in her skirt, a box of matches, too. The match flared and she inhaled, blowing the smoke sidelong out of her mouth.

'I only hope they won't be too pious and will let him play his little flute. Some music, you know? God, how I miss proper music.'

'He makes them work through the night,' I said. 'I see them. Sometimes I think I can hear them.'

'This far out?'

'I don't know. I think I can. When I'm in bed, I think I can hear voices around me, working, talking.'

'It's hard. But it's work. A balm.' Then: 'So you're still not sleeping.'

I felt exposed, a feeling compounded by our being on the roof. She was gazing at me with that ironic half-smile, but rushed to extinguish her cigarette at the sound of another bike clattering down the dirt track. It was Prince, Laxman's grandson. He usually came before sunrise, and we'd speak briefly while he deposited my new tiffin and collected the old one. He was a sparky, joyful boy with a fluffy moustache no wider than his nose. Though usually I looked forward to seeing him, I felt suddenly embarrassed that he'd turned up in her presence, that she'd learn that my meals were brought directly to my door, as if I considered myself royalty.

Prince didn't help matters: 'I bring food for our special guest!'

Radhika and I wandered down the stairs and into the yard, where Prince explained that he'd brought tomorrow's tiffin today because he was heading to Delhi later to apply for a Dubai visa.

'Oh, not you as well, Prince,' Radhika said. 'There's no alcohol there, you know.'

'Madam, as if I would!'

'Bring me back some perfume.'

'If you'll pray my visa is granted.'

'Daily.'

As I washed the old tiffin at the pump I saw Prince, who was still straddling his bike, jump forward off the saddle. 'Don't go in there, Madam!' he called, almost laughing.

Radhika looked back from where she'd been peering through the iron bars and into my room. 'Por que?'

'It's the china room.' He gave her a deep wink. 'It was for the women.'

'And what am I?'

'I'm joking, Doc! Go where you want. It's only that Baba told me how a woman was locked in there for doing' – he clicked his tongue knowingly – '*that* with someone who wasn't her husband.' His laughter dwindled as rapidly as water down a plughole when he caught my eye, calculating perhaps that if the story was true then this woman might have been someone to me. He left soon after, with our good wishes for his visa application, and I felt acutely that I needed to explain to Radhika that I didn't imagine myself to be – which didn't mean that I wasn't – some overindulged relative, and a British one at that, who expected to be waited on.

'I make my own tea,' I said, nodding at the outdoor mud-oven and the charred kindling.

'Really, what are you talking about?'

'Having this food' – I half-raised the tiffin in my hand – 'brought to my door. As if I was a king.'

'Or a prisoner. That was the first thought that popped into my head.'

I hadn't until then considered that my uncle might prefer to keep me away, that he wouldn't want me out in the bazaar, an embarrassment to be hidden. In the days I'd spent with Jai in his house, had people been coming up to him in the bank and asking about me and how ill I looked? About how much I stank of drink? Was I the cringe-worthy British relative?

Radhika was looking up to the roof. 'What a fucking waste – as if cigarettes aren't hard enough to come by,' she said, scowling. She wheeled her bicycle out of the gate, pointed it back down the track and climbed on, rearranging her skirt just so.

'Sunra's that way,' I said, gesturing in the opposite direction, and she looked at me so candidly I felt disarmed. She was beautiful, and appealing in the way that people unashamedly themselves always are. 'You said you only ever came this way if you were setting up a clinic.'

Her face broke into a massive grin. She took her broad-rimmed apricot hat, which I'd somehow not noticed before, from the white wire basket, secured it on her head and pedalled away, waving once she fell into a rhythm.

I waited until I could no longer see her, and then until my head had cleared, before taking out the results slip and looking at it properly. I'd flunked, as I'd expected. I hadn't turned up to two of my exams, too desperate to realise that I shouldn't be sweating in a park wood folding my sleeve up to my elbow when half a mile away my desk sat untaken, the paper unturned. So, no, I wasn't surprised at my marks, only sad at how disappointed my dad would have been as he collected the grade slips.

I thought how lucky I was to still be going to university, especially given my interview, when I'd jacked up in the toilets of Luton coach station on the way down to Victoria, hoping in vain that it would see me through the afternoon. It was my first time to the capital proper and everything seemed to pop with unreality: the classic Tube signs promising an underground world I was half-surprised to discover really existed; the sound of South Kensington, a name dripping with Royal icing; the light on the blond bricks of the Natural History Museum. After a speech by the faculty head, a tour of the maths department and a buffet lunch from which I grabbed more than most, we were shown to our plastic orange seats to await our turn. I didn't say much, though I wanted to. My feet were starting to itch, and then my shins ached, and I knew that soon my whole body would be rattling. I hugged my knees to my chest but when it felt like one of the other students was looking at me funny I put my legs back down. I went to the toilet. I still had half a bag left, wrapped in foil, but had thrown away my needle in Luton. So I pulled out my lighter and smoked it, sitting on the closed lid, the cubicle expanding with light.

By the time I was invited into Professor Nolan's office, I was awake but not present, my sensations, if not quite underwater, then certainly afloat across the lulling ocean of my mind.

'Sorry about the wait. If you might give me a moment.' Professor Nolan searched about his desk for my papers while I took in his big frame and comically pink face, which was full of broken capillaries. His white hair was swept back, revealing a widow's peak.

'Here it is,' he said, and repeated my name in his high Irish voice, making a hash of the pronunciation. He seemed speedily to absorb my personal statement. 'I see your masters expect great things from you.'

We called them teachers at my school but I didn't feel able to say that.

'Tell me a bit about yourself, then. What do you like about mathematics?'

'It's good to get an answer,' I said, after what felt like an hour.

'Yes. Yes, I suppose it is. Life can be quite indeterminate, can't it?'

He was smiling encouragingly and perhaps he expected me to go on, but I didn't, couldn't, my mind felt too soft, too cushioned, nothing was leaving an imprint, everything was settling back into plump nothings.

'Let's do something together, yes?' He scribbled a few equations down and slid the paper towards me, along with his pen. 'No rush. Take your time.'

The symbols were familiar, and I knew that if I could only focus I'd be able to prise out the answers. But my hands didn't leave my lap, his pen rolled off the desk, and something in my face prompted him to say:

'Too easy? Eager for the good stuff,' and he changed things up, adding some functions I didn't recognise, and pushed the paper back my way. 'Should be more up your street.'

I kept my body very still and turned only my head towards the paper. It made no sense. I said nothing, and he was looking at me much more closely now. I looked down at my hands and heard him slide the paper away.

'You say in your statement that you often visit India. Do you know Calcutta? Wondrous place,' and for the rest of our time together he told me the story of how he met his wife there, a fellow professor, when they were both in their fifties and getting on, and their plans to now spend half of every year in a bungalow just outside Ballygunge.

He was very matter-of-fact, abrupt, even, as he showed me out and called in the next candidate, and I felt despondent during the entire coach ride home. But then one Monday a few weeks later I got a letter saying that the university were delighted to make me an unconditional offer. I don't know why he did that, and I never saw or heard from him again, but it was such compassion, and from such an unexpected direction, that it lives with me to this day.

I lay the results slip on top of the kindling and sat by the oven with my chin on my knees, wondering how I'd cope with moving to London after the summer.

Very soon after her first visit, Radhika turned up again, cycling through the half-open gate and right into the courtyard. I was squatted over the latrine but could see her via the big cracks in the wooden door. She dismounted and leaned her bicycle by the porch, against one of the pillars. There were some things in the basket, too far away for me to identify. She ducked inside, briefly, then backtracked and looked through the iron bars of my room. Not finding me there, she headed over to the barn, clicking her fingers as she went, half-singing a song in a language unknown to me: *are rama krishna bane mani-hari/ odh li saree/ re hari.* It was a lovely, absent-minded sound, as if she wasn't even aware that she was singing, which made me feel that I'd witnessed something precious.

I started launching jugfuls of water down the latrine and she turned towards the cubicle and said, 'Sorry! I'll just wait here.' I came out determined not to look as sheepish as a man emerging from emptying his bowels only to be met with an amused woman pulling on a Marlboro.

'This is becoming a habit,' I said.

Her eyes flicked down to her cigarette. 'Oh, you mean my coming here! But, look, I come with colour.' She pulled something out from between the tins of paint in her basket. 'And a mirror. Now you can shave, no?'

'What's the paint for?'

'Your uncle, he said that if you're living here for free the least you can do is smarten the place up a bit.'

My uncle would never have said that, suggested that. Had she paid for all this? 'I'm not painting it.'

'Run off your feet, are you? I've brought brushes, too. And there are dustpans and brooms in there' – she was pointing at the barn – 'beside the old newspapers.'

I knew, of course, what she was doing: forcing me to focus, to give my mind a purpose and my days a shape. 'I'll think about it.'

'Glad we're on the same page. We'll need water.'

That first afternoon was all about preparation: removing flaking paint and debris from the walls and the pillars, sanding off gobbets of stone, washing down the yellow stonework with warm water. When I emptied the final bucket into the field and came back into the yard, she was wiping her face with the hem of her blouse, revealing one whole breast held in its cotton cup. Her skin was perfect and flushed and I put the bucket down at the pump and concentrated on refilling it.

Most mornings, once Prince had deposited the tiffin and before it was light enough to paint, I'd head up to the roof to see how far the workmen had got with the blue statue overnight. Sometimes I'd catch them still at it, their headlamps roving like fireflies. After a while, I'd move to the opposite wall, the one looking over the brown pen and away from the village, and through the green air I'd watch that boy in the far English school-field, avoiding the other schoolboys who kept tripping him up. There they were again, in the canteen, throwing white flour into his face. One morning, perhaps triggered by the distant building site, or even by Radhika's use of the word balm, which had lodged in my head, I saw him, nine years old. He was standing on the staircase, high on his tiptoes and peering through the spindles of the landing, and in again through his parents' open bedroom door. Dad had lifted his shirt to his neck and Mum was applying some kind of cream to his back. The recession had hit the little shop hard, and walking home from school I'd see Mum standing in the doorway, a long broom in her hand, wondering where the next customer might come from. To avoid selling up cheap, Dad had accepted work on a building site in Ealing, 150 miles away, living in someone's spare room during the week and coming home at the weekend to give Mum a break. The job required him to lift tall plastic tubs of bricks on to his back and carry them from one end of the site to the other, like some packhorse, for god knows how many hours a day and alongside mostly illegal immigrants. When he arrived home late on Fridays he had a difficult stiff gait as he handed me and my brother a present, usually a cassette of *Top of the Pops* hits. His back was scraped raw and covered with bleeding sores that had him flinching whenever Mum pressed in the ointment. She was trying hard not to cry, and Dad was staring straight ahead, trying equally hard not to think about his wife crying.

'How was this week?' Dad asked.

'A little better. I think we're turning a corner.'

Dad nodded. 'Customers okay?'

'Fine.'

'No more broken windows, I see. Must be good.'

'The best.'

'Honestly, no problems?'

'None, believe me.'

She was lying. I'd been on the settee earlier that evening when I'd heard the noise. I took my headphones off.
It was a woman, screaming at Mum, shouting that she
had no right to refuse her son alcohol. I moved towards
the wooden panel that opened into the shop, careful not
to be seen, and I listened to the woman loudly, so loudly,
itemise all the ways in which she was offended by my
mother's presence, all the ways in which she couldn't
stand the way my mother dressed and spoke and smelled.
When she left, slamming the door, I went back into the
living room, lay back on the settee, put back on my foamy
earphones and turned up the volume. I was staring at the
white ceiling. Why had they come here, to this broken,
white town? Had things really been so bad? There'd been
thirteen of us – uncles, aunts, cousins and all – in a two-
bed terrace near the centre of Derby, but at least the
neighbourhood was full of our own. And now those same
relatives, and more besides, were laughing, because my
parents had struck out together and were clearly not coping. I was raging at them, my parents. Mum walked in
and stood at the window, facing away from me and on to
the concrete yard. The back of her head was vibrating a
little. I turned towards her, but not enough to see her
reflection in the glass.

23

Suraj lies awake worrying about her. Desperate for news, he even risks asking Mai if her daughter-in-law is any better.

'Anything to avoid work,' she replies, which only sharpens his hatred. When he sees Mehar restarting her chores around the house, he hopes it's a sign that she's recovered from her illness, has perhaps even started to forgive him. He tries to catch her alone, but it's impossible, and so he reverts to life away from the farm, passing his days with friends in the shade of the masjid, pea-shooting stones into a spittoon, juggling rocks. Often, he'll ambush a cart on its way into the city (mollifying the protesting driver) and call at Kashyap's Vaishnu Dhaba, where every day you can get two chapattis from the tandoor and a bowl of fried lentils for not more than ten rupees a month. On his way home, he'll stop at the village crossroads, by a marble white Sikh temple being built, and join the circle of males gathered there. It is the only place you might get a decent signal, though even here the All India Radio announcer has to fight through the static. *Young men! Listen up, join the Youth Bharat Sabha! Fight for real freedom, not dominion status ...*

A small plant sits on top of the radio, and the volume pin is pitched so high the copper pot fits about.

'They don't know their shit from their piss,' Suraj says, to get the men going.

'Telling me. Weren't they asking us to join the farmers' collective? Is this youth one different?'

'Let the rich have their games.'

'Panditji's pushed his cock so far up the British arse he's got it stuck.'

'Quiet! Listen, won't you! Did he just say the Mussulmans are getting in on it, too?'

'Are you, Parveiz Miah?'

'Ask my wife, friend. I was the last to even know about my son's wedding.'

'And, pray tell, to which of your many wives should we pose the question?'

'Looking very tired lately, Parveiz Miah!'

Suraj breaks off from the laughter and continues along the asphalt, which is nothing more than a rugged avenue of leafless trees. Ahead, a soda-seller pushes his grubby three-wheeler, his vest stained with an arrow of sweat. Turning down an alley, Suraj spots a pink-bellied dog collapsed in the shade, resigned to the flies that hover above like a small raincloud. Her pregnant stomach rises and presses against the ground, radiating a kind of unseen heat, and Suraj imagines the warmth of the fur against his skin, and then all at once he is full of both dismay and gratitude because trailing that warmth – part of it, in fact – comes the memory of Mehar's hair in his hands. All the way down the alley he thinks of her, her hands on his back, her hot encouraging voice in his ear, her satisfied face when they'd finished. A voice. He turns round. It is Old Aunt Besant and she is waddling towards him as he stands there with the unmistakable tenting below his navel. He adjusts, cursing these bottoms and their stupid thin cotton.

'I've been calling and calling you,' Aunt Besant says, breathless. 'Should I be running, at my age?'

'Not with the volume you eat, mausi.'

'Scoundrel. Here' – she passes him a note, a yogi's prescription – 'read it for me. What's that thieving Brahmin saying now?'

He scans the blue scrawl. 'You need an injection of puréed cow-shit. Into your bum. Urgently.'

'By the lights of Nanak and all that is holy, tell me you're joking! It's a little ache in my bones, is all.'

'I wish I was, mausi. It sounds serious. Take this to the medicine-man now.'

She snatches it back, tucks it inside her sari blouse. She has a strange relationship with the village, this low-caste aunt. No one seems to either mind her or take her seriously. 'If I find out you're lying, I'm going straight to your mother, do you understand?'

'It says only the shit of pregnant cows. Don't let them get away with any sub-standard shit, will you?'

She frowns. 'Illness after illness. It spares no one. How is the daughter-in-law? Any better? Is it … ?' She mimes holding a baby. 'My daughter-in-law's the same. With child, I mean.'

Ridiculous village. Can't even be ill in peace. 'I wouldn't know. It's not my concern.'

'She looked awful taking the rotis out just now. I would have offered to help, in case your mother asks, but with my knees …'

'Of course, of course.'

Turning to go, she gestures to where his erection had been. 'I never knew your heart carried such feelings for me,' she laughs, and Suraj, blushing, begs his leave.

On the way back to the farm he climbs into one of the trees and finds a seat, straddling a rooty limb that has split thickly from the trunk, like a rival. There is nothing but fields all the way to the horizon, where the slate of blue sky takes over. Nothing at all but land and toil, and there she is, he is sure of it, piling the empty tiffins back into her basket, lifting the basket to her head. Arms elegantly holding on to her load, back straight, veil pulled down below her mouth, enough to allow her to catch her steps. He watches her wend through the bowing crops and all the time he is hoping for something to sprout up – a deserted little bunker, an unused watchtower – a place he could pull her to and where they would be undiscovered. So when he remembers the old parrot farm it feels like the blessing he is waiting for, and he is all but climbing down and running towards her when his face hardens, for she is already stepping out of the wheat and on to the dirt track, where Gurleen waits to accompany her home.

24

Later, he lies on the farmhouse roof, the ribbed mat rough against his back. There is camphor in the warm air and several hours until dawn. Everything is still. The china room is closed, the window slatted shut. He tips his head back. These stars. Precise and grand and so many it feels inscribed that he will be with her.

25

It has been so long since Suraj helped bring in the wheat that he rapidly falls behind the others and by the time the sun is in its high spot he is at least forty bundles from the nearest farmhand. Alone, he hacks away, a chop either side of the root, then a twisting out of the crop, the workers' far chatter like strings of silver on the hot breeze. His thighs ache, and there's a constant drip of sweat from his forehead, his nose, his chin. He pauses, mid-chop, on seeing her walk up the dirt track, the wide basket on her head. She pivots into the field and he watches her closing in, growing more real with every step, the sky so massive at her back it is as if she is descending from on high. The others receive their food first and then someone gestures towards him ('Don't forget the dragger') and he sees her look over from under her veil – she can't have made out his face from that distance – and follow the soil-path round, describing a full semicircle until she is but a few feet away. She lifts the basket from her head and holds it out to him, so he might pick his two rotis and whatever daal he fancies with his own hands, without any risk of touching her flesh.

'Take some water, too, brother. It's a hot day.'

It is the first time Mehar has spoken to him since she discovered the lie, and it transpires he's been so desperate to meet her again there has been no space to feel embarrassed; until now, when the shame of his deception washes over him and robs him of speech. He lifts the small bowl of water and tentatively places his hand on top of hers. There's an audible catch in her throat.

'How are you feeling now?' He cannot see past her veil.

A long silence. She takes her hand back. 'Spare my life, I beg you, please.'

'You're not sparing mine.'

'Don't try to speak to me.'

'That's a very severe punishment.'

'If I could string you up from the barn, I certainly would.'

'For loving you?'

'You've ruined me.'

'No one's ruined anyone,' he says, giving in to impatience. 'No one knows a thing. Not Mai. Not anyone.'

'This isn't a game. You don't get to play with my honour.'

'Listen to yourself. Ruin. Honour. People need to stop thinking in such small ways. The world is changing.'

155

Irritably, as if she were being needlessly unreasonable, he takes out his food and drops the empty tiffin back into the basket – 'I'm done' – and she bends her knees to lift the thing on to her head. 'You were betrothed to me, you know. We were meant to be married. But when he saw you, he changed it all round.'

'It's decided. You can't change the past.'

'But that's just it! You can. We can. We can have whatever we want. And I want you.'

Later, she'll wonder if that is the essence of being a man in the world, not simply desiring a thing, but being able to voice that desire out loud.

'I've put a paper in the tiffin.' About to leave, she hears amusement in his voice that infuriates and halts her. 'A timetable for meeting by that abandoned parrot farm towards Sunra. I'll see you there.'

She twists round, torso only, and the hot breeze grips her veil, sucking it to her lips so she must spit it out before she can speak. 'I think if it had been Gurleen you had been betrothed to, but me you'd ended up marrying, then it would be her standing here, not me.'

'That's not true. You can't think that.'

'No, no. Of course I can't. Only you can tell me what to think.'

She fishes out the timetable and folds it into her underwear before stepping out of the field and on to the dirt road.

'You were a while with the last worker,' Gurleen says, as they continue down to the farm.

'He took a long time emptying the tiffin.'

'Who?'

'I wouldn't know.'

'It seemed you did,' Gurleen presses.

'Then I hope Mai didn't catch you with your veil up,' says Mehar.

26

Mehar is illiterate, so the paper contains nothing but images: a row of boxes drawn in a hand unused to holding a pen, and within the boxes are suns, some in ascendance, some at the peak of their arc, a few near-set. There are also many boxes that he's kept empty, which, she figures, must represent those days on which he's calculated they won't be able to meet. It staggers her to imagine how closely he has been watching her, the attention paid to the rhythm of her days. She refolds the paper many times, secures it inside the thin panel of her underwear, and continues with the evening's chores: shelling peas, sweeping the roof, scrubbing the stone bath from the inside.

She knows she will go, if only to deflect the anger he might unleash if she were to stay away. He might tell her husband about them. Tell Mai. He'd be fine, his part in it all downplayed, even conveniently justified. Men have their needs. But for her life would be over. She can see herself now: head shaved, breasts exposed, the iron pig-ring around her neck and the coarse rope parading her through the village. She can hear the crowds calling her a dirty whore and feel the rocks cutting her flesh as she lurches to the well and jumps to her drowning end. Yes, for those reasons she will go. But, lying on her bed, her back to Harbans' back, she recognises another note, a lighter, brighter music behind the crashing death-cymbals. She listens to it, and hears it for what it is: desire, her own, amplifying. She closes her eyes and whispers, out loud but so only she can hear it – 'I want you, too' – and then she reopens them, and for a long time she stares at the muddy apples spilled across the stone ledge of the window.

*✱✱

The paint Radhika had brought me was a very light shade of pink, almost white, the colour of a ballet slipper. It matched what had been there before, judging by the few flakes still clinging to the pillars. One afternoon I was working outside the gate, priming the exterior wall, when a man arrived on a silver Bajaj scooter. He wore one of those black half-face sixties helmets, with a large flip-up visor, and it took him an age to unclip it from under his chin and head towards me. I'd not met him before and I didn't stop my work to meet him now.

'You're sensible to leave this wall until it's in shade.'

There was grey in his wavy combed-back hair, as much grey as black, and the same was true of his goatee, though that seemed more of a vanity, a trimmed and lustrous Vandyke. He looked like he might have once played in a band, like he still jammed with his friends at the weekends now that they all sported pot bellies, now that helmets didn't quite clasp under their chins as easily as they once had. The kind of guy who'd been certain he'd belong to the future. In reality, I soon learned, he was a teacher of Commerce and Society at Hindu Kanya High School, the local – secular, despite the name – secondary for girls. He was unmarried and lived alone in the neighbouring village, Sunra, up the dirt track and in a house with a gunny sack for a door.

'Tanbir,' he said, extending a hand. 'You're making good progress.'

'Let's hope the progress is making me.'

He gave a small gruff laugh. I went back to coating the wall in watery primer. It seemed of poor quality and I doubted if it would make any difference to the finish.

'Jai's done well,' he said. 'A house-sitter and a fixer-upper in one.'

I said nothing. I felt discomfited by his easy confidence, by how at home he seemed to be, and wanted him to turn around and go, taking the helmet he'd left dangling off the scooter's handlebar.

'The last time I saw your uncle he was replacing the heater in the bank. Always rushing round doing something, that man. Gosh, that must have been – two years ago? Winter-time. How is he keeping? Well?'

'Think so.'

Jai hadn't once been here since dropping me off on that first day, nearly three weeks earlier, and Tanbir must have sensed something of my confusion because he said,

'Like I say, he's a busy guy. But I hope your aunt's looking after you?'

At this I stood and looked at him face on. Visitors never asked about my aunt and I wondered what lay behind his question. 'I'm fine.'

'How are you coping without electricity?'

'It's not a problem.'

'Dr Chaturvedi's keeping an eye on things?'

Again he surprised me. I think my lips moved, but nothing came out. Who was this man? Radhika had been here again the previous day to drop off more paint, a new roller. We'd shared some whisky from her flask. I didn't know what to say to him and my hands went to my waist, in confrontation.

'Look.' His tone changed, became conciliatory, even confiding. 'People are beginning to whisper. That she's here a lot, an out-of-stater on this lonely farm with a young boy half her age. I thought you should know.'

'Shouldn't you be telling this to her, not me?'

'I did.'

I waited.

'She – she hooted, really, and said I had a tiny, tiny mind.' He smiled, rueful. 'She thinks she's Isabel fucking Archer. But she doesn't know what it's like round here. She thinks she does. But she doesn't, not really. If they take against someone, they'll eat her alive, slowly, from the inside.' He looked down, then across to his scooter. 'I should make a move. Would you mind if I called again someday?'

'It's a free country,' I said, and he laughed, wagging a finger as if to show he knew I was making some awful joke.

Radhika stopped by often, to check how I was getting on, to help with the painting, or sometimes simply to talk. The more she came, the more I wanted her to stay, and the more I started to feel for her. The morning after Tanbir's visit, I was looking out from the roof, hoping to see her, and suddenly there she was, turning towards the farm, waving. She joined me on the roof, standing right beside me, and we watched the work on the Krishna statue up ahead. The legs, a pair of thick blue columns, pressed together, were complete. A blue torso, too. A web of ropes tethered the thing to the ground. Constructors milled. Trucks came and went. In one, its rear panel swinging open, lay a gigantic blue arm, palm cupped towards the sky as though it were pointing out the two bright green parakeets flying overhead.

'Who's Isabel Archer?' I said.

Radhika crossed her arms loosely and exhaled, and I felt her shoulder touch mine. 'A clever girl in a novel. Ends up— Why?'

I didn't know how to explain. 'No reason.'

She looked at me closely. 'It's an idea, you know. You should read. It'll help you pass the time.'

I'd picked up a book at the airport, one I hadn't started yet but was eager to; as if I hoped reading about life might be a way to overcome it. 'Yeah, maybe.'

'I can bring you some. What're you into?'

I didn't know that yet. 'Anything. I don't mind.'

We embarked on my task for the day, which was painting the porch, staying out of the midday heat. Radhika took one end, I the other. Suddenly she waved her paint roller at me. 'That washed-up teacher. Has he been talking to you?'

I stopped painting. 'Who?'

'He likes his books and whatnot. Probably wanks over James. Has he? Been here?'

'Who's James?'

'Long hair. Beard. Middling height. Fat cheeks.'

'James?'

'I believe his name's Tanbir Singh.'

I shrugged, admitting defeat. 'He came to say people were talking about you.'

'Ha! I knew it! I knew he would! He takes his job way too far. He thinks he walks some moral high ground looking down on us all, throwing out advice.'

Still, I couldn't help noticing that she was far from outraged. Humming to herself, she moved the roller through the tray of paint, once, twice.

'I assumed you were from the city?' I said, keen to continue the conversation.

'What made you think that?'

'I don't know. You live there, don't you?'

'For now.'

'And before?'

'Before?'

'Where are you from?' I said, already exasperated.

'I'm from Ranchi, which is the capital city of the state of Jharkhand. A very long way away.'

'So how did you end up here?'

She reached quietly for her cigarettes then thought better of it. Worried I'd hurt her, I tried to think of something light-hearted to win her back.

'Should you really be smoking around me? Offering me whisky? It's a pretty slippery slope I'm on.'

As if I'd not even spoken, she stepped towards me, looking serious, and I thought we might kiss, something I wanted very much and, now it seemed possible, felt completely unprepared for. 'I had all this anger,' she said, 'all this resentment and energy that had no good outlet. And then I found my outlet and things improved.'

'Your outlet? Like a pipe?'

'My work, doofus. Medicine. Look alive.'

I smiled. 'Sorry. And you come here to help me find my outlet? Like you did?'

'I don't think I can do that,' she said. 'That's all on you,' she added, and I nodded, because it was true. 'But I do find this place a haven.'

'I think my mum loved it growing up.'

'It's a respite from …' She gestured beyond the farm. 'Plus it's a nice change to spend time with a young man who doesn't judge me too much.'

'You know I was joking about smoking around me and …' But she was smiling. 'I'm glad you come here,' I said. 'Thank you.'

'Please don't. There's no need.'

She kissed my cheek and brushed past my arm, and I watched her walk back to her side of the porch. I felt a sharp longing for her, and beside that longing, faith that life need not remain a wail of anger, that it can also be full of beautiful moments that just seem to arrive with the birds.

Prince, who liked to talk, had told me some of the village stories about Radhika: she was in hiding from a drug lord she'd double-crossed; she'd been struck off in Bihar for killing a politician's daughter during an appendectomy; she was a divorcee who'd abandoned her child to run off with a man twice her age, a man who'd later dumped her in a snow-capped chalet in Shimla. On that day we painted the porch, she told me everything herself. She was born in Patna, the daughter of a clever, frustrated Bengali mother and a charming Bihari drunk. When Radhika was six, her mother left her violent husband and crossed into West Bengal, where the two of them lived, on sufferance, in a single side room in the house of some extended family. Three years later, Radhika's mother boarded a train for Ranchi with a man who was exactly twice her age, with plans to set up a new school. Radhika was to remain with the extended family, until her mother and her partner were ready for her to start upper primary in her new home. *And wouldn't that be much better, Radhu?* She did join her mother in Ranchi, but not until she was twelve and a much older cousin had, the night before her departure, tiptoed into her room and slid under the floral sheet. The new school hadn't worked out and her mother waited tables at night and sold face creams by day. She'd left her partner, who'd turned out to be just another abusive drunk, but when Radhika's mother began shitting blood and was diagnosed with cancer of the bowel, they arrived at the old man's doorstep and he, beaming with awful benevolence, allowed them in. It was a slow death. She lasted six years, with only the most rudimentary treatment. Less than two months after Radhika cast her mother's ashes into the Subarnarekha, the old man, now seventy, put his hand on her breast. She'd been studying at the time, and he came up behind her, one hand on her shoulder and began stroking her nipple through her shirt. She smiled up at him and led him to the bedroom, where she tied his wrists to the bedstead. He looked terribly excited. His arm was whorled in thick white fur and before Radhika had even finished spraying the deodorant and got out her lighter, he was screaming, blowing on his arm and calling her a nothing little slut. She grabbed her textbook, her bag, and left, first to Goa and then to take up her sponsored medical studies in Hyderabad.

I nodded, unsure what to say. It was sundown and she looked off to the sky.

When she turned thirty, she continued, she decided to get out of the cities and do some fieldwork. It took a while for the right opportunity to arrive, one that didn't require her to fellate anyone on the appointing committee, but then a role in some godforsaken back-water of Punjab appeared on the staff noticeboard. It was a one-year trial to investigate whether having a large presence of female doctors made any difference to rates of female infanticide, a metric on which Punjab leads the way. She got the nod and had a heaving goodbye party where she laughed and got drunk and smoked dope and sobbed with her friends. And then she got here, one boiling afternoon, and quickly realised Dr Duggal resented her mere existence and wasn't going to let her establish anything more than a roving monthly clinic where she could hand out soft yellow leaflets on the various types of birth control. She only came to my uncle's house that time because Duggal had been complaining about having to go and see what some foreign prat had gone and done to himself, and she was so bored she'd insisted on tagging along.

'I'm glad I did,' she said, standing up.

I wanted to touch her so much, for us to be together and close all night, but we walked to the gate in silence.

On his second visit, Tanbir brought a bag of peas, freshly picked.

'Hungry?' he called, holding aloft the thin blue bag. 'I thought you might be sick of greasy dhaba food.'

When I said nothing he came through the gate, his smiling face emerging abruptly from the explosion of sunlight on metal. He looked at the house, across its newly painted façade. 'Good job. Nearly finished?'

'Nearly.'

'Inside still needs doing.'

'You reckon?'

His face changed, now weary, as if he had to put up with enough of these ironic inflections in the classroom.

'I don't have anything to cook the peas with,' I offered, conceding a little.

We sat on the charpoy shelling the peas with our thumbnails and eating them straight from the pod. He told me about Sunra, a place of steep cobbled lanes and a couple of hundred stone houses. He'd been born there, he said, which surprised me for some reason. I'd had him down as a big-city do-gooder come to help the poor folk. But, no, he'd never lived anywhere else and now, since his father's stroke, that didn't look like it could change.

'Where is your father?'

'In a care facility. Towards the city. I go to see him every other day,' he added defensively.

'So you mean you've never really left?'

'Only to get my teaching diploma. And then I came back.'

'I hope you love your work.'

He said he did, very much.

'And being alone?'

'It has its charms, for sure.'

'Why didn't you get married?' I asked, as if, at forty, that option was long gone.

'I choose not to discuss that.'

I smiled a little and nodded, acknowledging the moment without extending it. There was a small silence.

Then: 'I saw your aunt yesterday,' he said, with the air of someone trying to drag the conversation on to more familiar terrain.

'Oh?'

'She was in the bazaar. With her little boy. She seemed happy?'

I said nothing. I felt enough loyalty to my uncle not to gossip about the state of his marriage.

'I don't mean to pry,' he said.

We heard the rattle before the bell ting-a-linged and Radhika rode into the yard. I was elated that she'd turned up, though I tried not to let that show on my face.

'You finished the mouldings!' she said.

'I found a ladder in that back field.'

She left aside the bike and perched, rod-straight, on the end of our charpoy, her knees crossed under her long skirt. She took a fat pod from the tray and traced her nail around the bumps. 'Have you come to keep an eye on us?' she said to Tanbir.

He showed his palms in apology. 'I'm sorry I misspoke.'

'You come in peas,' she said, and we chuckled, though most of my delight was in her use of 'us', as if we were a unit apart from everyone else.

She roped Tanbir into helping us clean out the inner rooms and soon we all had brooms in hand and were sweeping the thick dust across the porch and on to the courtyard. We broke up the cot and busted charpoys and set the wood aside to use as kindling, but the rest of the rubbish – the tins of Ovaltine, the piles of old calendars, the smashed earthenware pots and willow-pattern shards, the boxes of rusted bent nails – we dumped outside the gate. There were still holes in the walls, but I'd discovered some enamel bricks in a corner of the barn and thought they could be used to fill the gaps. Radhika offered to bring a hammer and some cement the next day, and Tanbir said he knew someone who'd collect the scrap from the gate. We washed at the pump, watering our faces and arms, and then, exhausted more by the sullen heat than by actual labour, we returned to the charpoy. It was evening and our shadows lengthened over the yard, black on gold, stretching as the sun dipped behind the plane trees. Radhika lit up. I declined, but when Tanbir accepted I reached for one too, and she smiled a little, and I wished I'd not given so much away.

Silence pervaded, the long day's ordinary quiet. For once, I hadn't rolled my sleeves down from my shoulders, and I watched the sweat beading my arms. I thought how I wasn't stammering any more. That my sleep had improved. And I realised that this was what I liked, not being on my own, far from it, I wanted people around me, I just didn't want to talk. I wanted undemanding friendships, transcendent connections, all and forever on my own terms. I ground out my cigarette and, without asking, took a second from the carton.

There was another evening tugging at the back of my mind; quietly I let it come. I was upstairs in my room, trying to get on with my GCSE homework, my curtains shut against the older schoolkids who gathered outside the shop. They were always there, the older kids, with their grey threatening noise, and there was constant fear in my heart that things might flare up, as they often did. I heard my dad labouring up the stairs and I reached round in my seat and opened the door.

'You okay, Dad?'

'Just lying down.' He was grimacing with every step, a hand to his lower back.

'You don't look good,' but he waved me away and entered his room.

By two in the morning he was in the bathroom crying out in pain. I knocked on the door. 'Dad, what's the matter? Open up!'

When he unlocked the door and came out his face was wet with what I thought was water but then realised was sweat. It was running down his arms.

'I'm calling an ambulance.'

He looked at me aghast. He was so removed from any idea that he might not be able to sort something out by himself, that he might have to impose on someone else. 'It's just a muscle,' he said and limped back into his room.

I heard his alarm go off at five as normal and listened to him struggle down the stairs, where he'd carry in the newspapers and sort out the deliveries. By the time I came down in my school uniform he was trying to lift the six-packs of milk that had just arrived. His breathing was hard.

'Dad? Please?'

'Get to school,' he managed, before dropping the milk and collapsing to the floor.

I went with him in the ambulance. The doctor, a young Asian guy, said it was a pulmonary embolism, a blood clot, that he should have come in straight away and was lucky to be alive. Years of high blood pressure. High stress, he'd added, as if all this was somehow Dad's fault. When the doctor left, Dad gestured to my tie and wondered if it was too late for me to get to school. I didn't reply. I put my hand on his brow and didn't say anything at all.

Perhaps that was my first proper inkling that this place, this town, this estate, would kill us, but it would be another three months before I fully understood. Dad was still recovering, on daily blood thinner, though he'd already dismissed my mother from the shop and installed himself back behind the counter. One sunny afternoon, in the middle of my exams, I was walking home through Ringwood Park after sitting my history paper. Halfway down our street, the shop came into view. An ambulance was parked outside and I ran to it I ran to it I ran to him.

He'd been beaten up by two men, two men who didn't steal anything, who only wanted to inflict violence on a middle-aged brown man. The paramedics were tending to his arms, but it was his face that was bloodied, his nose broken, his eyes already swelling shut. I remember the blood rising through his moustache and covering his lips and teeth. The bubbles of it and Dad trying to spit it out. Around two weeks later, on my way home from my summer job in a laundry, I recognised Dad's white van parked up on a side street around the corner from where we lived. He was sitting inside, on the driver's seat, the engine cut, and his head was down, as if he was praying, except I knew Dad never did that. He looked so quiet, solemn, sad. White stitches still under his eyes. What was he thinking? Did he think he'd made the right decision in coming here? To this town? To England? Did he wonder, like I did, like I still do whenever I see my daughter be so casually, so unthinkingly, sidelined in the playground, did he too wonder if these people would ever agree to share ownership of this land? Did he worry that our lives here would always be seen as fundamentally illegitimate? I think of Dad in that moment, sitting in that van, in that pose, so often. It is like a drug, that memory, one I keep needing to return to no matter the hurt it brings. When lying in bed or writing an email or bundling the kids out of the car and back into the house, I'll suddenly think of it, of Dad all alone with his private pain, and all I can do is shut the door on the kids and go into another room and wait for the feelings to pass through me. I watched Dad for many minutes and he did not once move. I didn't want him to see me, but I knew if I went straight home, he would arrive soon after, laughing, smiling, his sadness tucked away. I found that thought unbearable. I swear I would have grabbed a knife and driven it through my shaking wrist. So I didn't go home. I took myself off to

Ringwood Park, where I stayed all evening, until the cars arrived and some older kids who'd left my school the previous year rolled down their window. They'd offered me smack plenty of times in the past but this time I got in the car, added a tenner to the pile, and once they'd scored we drove to a filthy flat on the same estate as my school and I watched them fight over who would get the first hit.

27

The wheat is cloaked in sleeves of red and apricot and a nightjar perches watchfully on the well, jerking its head this way and that. The bird seems rooted to its own shadow, plumage fiery in the sunset, until it spots a moth and, in no especial hurry, unfurls its graceful wings and pushes up into the air. Had there been anyone there to observe it, they would surely have marvelled at the animal's long and single-minded attack, at the perfect parabola it described as it swooped around the stone hut. But, no, there is no one there to observe the spectacle. All is quiet in the village of Sunra. Children are being rocked to sleep, milk is bubbling in brass pots, men are washing off the mud of the day. And inside the old parrot farm's disused stone hut (as the nightjar passes unnoticed overhead) Mehar is unhooking her tunic from the metal peg while Suraj lies naked on the stone floor, lighting a roll-up. It is the fourth time they have met like this and she can feel the intensity of his gaze as the cotton of the tunic slips like running water down her body. She steps into her bottoms and yanks tight the drawstring.

'I'll get a job,' he says, and it is almost disappointing, the revelation that it is not, after all, a deep appreciation of her beauty that has rendered him silent these last few minutes, that his mind has only been stolen by more practical concerns.

'If you want,' she says.

'Then we'll move. To a big city far away. One we can get lost in. Lahore, I think. It won't take me long to save enough.'

Such confidence! As if the world only existed to be cowed in the face of his youth and courage. She is five years younger but sometimes feels so much the elder, so much the one who can think ahead, foresee obstacles.

'I can start putting things aside,' she says. 'Things we'll need. And we should go before the rains, before the roads flood again.'

'That gives us three months, yes? Three months.' He is adamant. He sits up, roll-up dangling from the rim of his lower teeth. He is looking up to the window, at the square of purpling sky. In that moment, Mehar sees what he sees, a country beyond convention, a life beyond the walls of the china room. How much of her love for him is bound up with this promise of freedom? Guilt creeps up on her, confusing her, and she looks away from him.

'I'll think of a story,' she says. 'Something we can say to the people of Lahore.'

He keeps his gaze on the window. 'We can say what we want. And does it matter anyway? Does it matter what they think?'

'In time it will matter. When it comes to marrying our children it will matter. They'll want to know our background. Who our ancestors are. The world isn't so modern yet, you know.'

'The world will be completely different by then.' He turns to her, his eyes full of hot certainty. 'We'll make it different.'

Both dressed, he helps her with her wicker basket of red chillies.

'One thing,' he says, as she steadies the load on to her head-cushion. 'Has he restarted his visits?'

'Not really,' she says, after a small silence. She doesn't say how tender his brother now is with her, that when she complains of still feeling unwell he never insists and instead tells her to rest, that children can wait.

'Well. Be careful.'

She turns and drops the veil so he might not see the anger on her face. Be careful. As if she could do anything to stop it. 'Why?' she says, her voice all bite. 'Would you not bring up another man's child, you modern-modern man?'

'Don't be foolish.'

'Are you still enjoying your wife's company?'

'Barely. For appearances' sake.' He reaches for her hand. 'Would you have her complain to Mai again?'

'I think we've established that what I'd have doesn't matter.'

She wakes up feeling surly and irritable, something of their spat having carried over into the morning. Perhaps that's why she's overslept, because already the tea has been made, the dough kneaded, and there is no sign of her sisters. She lies back, sighs. Closes her eyes. She hears a cart coming down the track: the clop of the horse, a man imploring his son to put down his silly slingshot and listen, that being a watchmaker requires attention. In Lahore, Mehar thinks, she will have a watch, a timepiece that she will carry around the city, a city she will walk through freely, her face uncovered. Sitting up again, she hears voices in the yard and puts her eye to the slats. It is Gurleen, upset and being comforted by Mai. Though there is something odd about the comfort Mai is offering, something too insistent, too lingering in the way she is pressing Gurleen's arm, her shoulder. Gurleen, too, looks unsure, hesitant. A memory flares – Mai's hard hands, Monty's sobbing embrace – but is immediately quashed by Gurleen's entrance.

'What's happened?' Mehar asks. 'What's got you so upset?'

Gurleen takes up the dough.

'I said what's happened?'

'Nothing. Children. I'm sad I'm not in that way yet.'

A pause while Mehar watches her, decides that that makes sense. 'We all feel like that. Give it time.'

28

Suraj secures a job as an apprentice sign painter in Mission bazaar, the main thoroughfare in the city. He pushes his rented two-wheeled cart of rented materials – ladders, brushes, stencils, heavy buckets of coloured powders – all day long, from one end of the vast market to the other. By the time he returns the equipment to the warehouse, his shoulders are cramping so much that it is all he can do to lift his hand and collect his payment.

'There isn't work enough around here?' Mai says, as he washes the green dye from his neck and arms, from the brown trunks of his legs, looking for all the world like a shedding tree.

'I want to be paid for my labour,' he replies.

Mohan has to pump the water because Suraj lacks the strength, and then he kneads life back into his younger brother's shoulders. Watching from the window of the china room, the pearls in her fist, Mehar has an odd, spacey realisation that she will leave this place without ever speaking a word to the middle son, Harbans' husband, that there has always been too much formality for them ever to express anything to one another. The strange thought dissolves the moment Suraj rises, and when he hobbles over the courtyard and disappears into one of the inner chambers, she finds a handkerchief, makes a parcel of the pearls and hides it inside her tunic, against her breasts.

At the hut the following morning, Mehar rests the buckets in the slanting shade and steps indoors, where he is waiting, once again looking out of the window.

'What took you so long?'

'I had to deliver the milk.' She doesn't mention that it was a task Gurleen had foisted on her; that would only sour their time together.

Afterwards, he lies there on his stomach, walking his fingers over the fine notches along her hipline, indentations left by the tight panel of her salwar. How neat, how soft, these little ridges of flesh. He runs his tongue over them.

Outside, something stirs in the wheat.

She reaches under the pile of her tunic, for a parcel of some sort.

'And what do I do with these?' he asks, as the pearls slither into a heap on the flat of his palm. 'I'll get some strange looks if I wear them to work.'

'Sell them,' she says, head popping through the neck of her tunic, arms wriggling into place. 'Add it to the money you're saving. We'll get to Lahore that much sooner.'

'I'm working now.'

'And don't you just make sure everyone knows it! Crawling to your room. Complaining of your aches. Sell them and save us our pity.'

'And Mai?'

'She's never asked me about them yet. Then we'll be gone.' She can tell he's not convinced and decides to press him. 'I don't even like them. White's not my colour.'

'What is your colour?' he asks, humouring her.

She thinks. 'Red. Pink, maybe. Yes, light pink. Buy me some pink jewels in Lahore.'

'You've already got a lovely pink jewel,' he says, and she spins round, shock on her face.

29

A few clothes. Maybe two pairs. The green cotton and, in case of cold weather, the chequered twill. Her wedding shawl, too. She's not leaving that behind. Though she shouldn't take too many things. They'll need to be light on their feet. They'll be travelling by night. *By beautiful moonlight they'll make their escape, disappearing into the silver abroad.* Lines from where, she cannot remember. A parent maybe. Her father? Tallow sticks. Yes. A knife. Fruit. Perhaps she could hide some rotis from the evening meal. Inside her shawl. So, yes, maybe she will take her shawl. It's a long journey. He'll probably wear a shawl too. Or a blanket over his head. He'll be cold. Will he be cold? Some oil to massage his feet. Walking so much. Walking there. Will he find work there? A new life. With him. Only him. What a temper he has. But I know not to stand it. To control it. His blessings in my ear and I will wash my face with the dust at his feet. The lightning of his touch. My pink jewel! Wedding jewels. Mai's trunk. If only. How they'd help once they got to Lahore. How to get the key, how to get … A small bag. She could start hoarding these things in the hut – or, nearer, in the field? – ready for the day. Oh, God, oh my Lord, please protect us. Lead me out of here safely. Me in my shawl, he in his blanket, setting out over the road and out of this village. Out out out. Please protect us. Show us mercy.

'You're going to ruin the life out of that,' Gurleen says, and, apologising, Mehar lifts the wick out of the melted tallow. 'Too busy daydreaming these days, you are.'

'I'm working. Don't push me.'

'Working?' Gurleen says archly. 'Is that what they call it?'

'Stop it!' Harbans snaps, pleads. 'Can't we just do our work? Please!'

Mehar dips the wick back into the fat. And then, because they will be left behind and part of her twists in guilt at every sight of Gurleen: 'How are you anyway? Can I help?'

'Wretched things,' Gurleen replies, from the charpoy. She is still applying mint leaves to her forearms, where the wasps did their worst.

'Where do you keep coming across them?'

'They deserve to die,' Gurleen says, and looks over to Harbans, sieving lentils, her hand shaking.

*

185

They are in bed, and all is silence when the door opens, without so much as a knock. They sit up at once, and then Gurleen stands, as if she'd somehow been expecting Mai at this hour. She has a small lantern in her hand, and shadows vault up the wall.

'I heard something about wasps,' says Mai. 'How are things now?' A pause. 'Still the same?'

'Yes. Still the same.'

'Well,' Mai says, turning away. 'It's your own fault.'

30

Afternoon torpor and a giant, male-sounding knock on the gate. Mai, dredged up from her nap, emerges to see five men, armed.

'And?' she says, unbowed.

'I want to speak to the head.'

'So speak.'

The brothers set out the chairs, find the table, and when the main man sits he plants the rifle between his outspread legs, the barrel of the gun leaning against a thigh. He has an Italian moustache, ends curling and slicked up to a great shine, and only the lightest of beards, as if this were a fine hammock holding up his head. His eyes are long and bright, lashed like a woman's. An elegant face. Only his hands betray something rougher: hard yellow bulbs all along the seam where palm meets fingers. It does look heavy, the rifle. His name, as the whole state knows, is Tegh Singh.

'Your sons like to observe,' Tegh Singh says, bringing his tea-glass down.

'They take their cues from me,' Mai replies. Legs spread too, hands on her knees and elbow jutting out like a tea-pot. She twists the reed of straw in her mouth.

'It is a good thing, to observe. To always be watching, questioning. It's the way ideas develop.' He graces Suraj with a smile. 'It's ideas that make revolutions. That will make this one.'

Suraj looks away, off into the blandishments of the sky. He doesn't want to meet the man's gaze, to engage with him. This struggle, this fight, is not what he feels he is about, is not about him at all, a twenty-year-old who has yet to talk to a white man.

'Purna swaraj,' Tegh Singh goes on. 'We will settle for nothing less. Complete self-rule. It will take time, but not too much. Because I can hear the new India breathing. I can hear her waiting for us to raise her on to our shoulders and up to the light. It will take sacrifices. There will be those who die in the fight. But we must all be prepared to take on our burdens.'

An oft-repeated little speech, by the sounds of it. Jeet shows three fingers to Mohan, who promptly detaches from the group and returns with a small brown parcel for Mai.

'Three sons,' Tegh Singh says. 'Perhaps one might join us? Join the fight? We're planning an attack and, let me say, mother, we need men more than money.'

'I'm not in the business of giving up my sons. At least not yet,' she adds, smiling at her boys. 'And only a fool would turn away money. You're not that, are you? May this help your cause,' she finishes, passing the notes on.

'It is all our cause,' he says, a little too earnestly for Suraj, who suppresses a laugh.

Like everyone else, they'd been expecting him. The whole village had been a-chatter with the news that the great Tegh Singh was in and around the city, assembling funds to launch an attack on the British. Funds or men, the rumour went. So you'd better make sure you had the funds.

'So where is this new India he mentioned? Is it as far as the river?' Mehar asks.

'It's just another idea,' Suraj says. 'That it's better to be oppressed by your own than by the British. It won't change anything for us.'

They are on their sides and Mehar comes up behind him to rest her cheek between his shoulder blades.

'In Lahore, where will we live?'

'I'll find somewhere. I promise.'

There is silence. She imagines the village crashing into the hut and catching them like this, her arms around him, his hands on hers. She'd almost welcome it.

'Can you imagine if they caught us like this?' he says, and Mehar, dumbstruck, blinks several times.

'Old Aunt Besant came looking for you yesterday,' she says, eventually. 'Told me she had a very special effect on you. She also said she's going to make *you* have injections in your bum next time.'

He doesn't laugh, barely makes a noise of assent, and in the quiet a phrase Tegh Singh uttered swims towards her.

'Complete self-rule,' she whispers, not loud enough for anyone else to hear, as though the idea were a wonderful heresy.

There's a sudden noise, a movement in the crops that freezes them both. Stealthily, Suraj shifts on to his knees, his feet, and edges to the door, certain he is prepared to kill whomever it may be. But it is only a dog, a thin black stray bouncing high in the gold of the wheat. The relief of it makes Suraj laugh, and loudly.

'Come and look at this,' he says, and they stand in the doorway watching the happy animal yap and jump, yap and jump.

'What's that?' Mehar asks, of the thing trailing around the dog's neck.

It is a string of red bunting, in all likelihood from some festival, and Suraj retrieves it from the bouncing animal and coils it around Mehar's head, a crown of sorts. She spends a moment rearranging it all, so the bunting trails through her hair like a corsage. She can't stop touching it.

'What do you think?' she asks, though she is not facing him. She is still at the doorway, looking out, he behind her.

'My queen.'

'When I am free this will be my hair every day. You agree, my lord?' she asks, glancing over her shoulder, and Suraj, hand across his heart, bows low.

31

It is washing day, Lord knows where the other two have got to, and Mehar's shoulder is tiring under the sodden roll of the indigo sheet. She stretches and squares it out along her arm, then launches it across the line. As she bends to take up another, she finds herself wondering how long it's been since she last bled. She tries to think – can she even remember? – when from inside the china room comes the sound of shattering, smashing. Mehar throws the wet sheet back into the basket and hurries there. She sees Mai sitting on one of the beds. At the long cement slab, bewilderingly, is Jeet, his back to Mehar. His shoulders are shaking, and on the ground are the broken shards of Mai's wedding plates. Mehar pulls down her veil.

'They fell,' Mai tells her.

'I'll clean it up,' Mehar says, as Jeet exits the room, and through the bottom of her veil she watches Mai leaving too, her feet stepping through the shards, stepping on them.

32

Suraj is at the top of his ladder when the calls for prayer come and the cobbles of the tight lane below disappear beneath ten, fifty, one hundred, two hundred men coming out of their stores, reaching for their cotton caps, heading towards the masjid. The white caps are like silken buoys on a surging river. Twice his ladder is jostled and Suraj grips the roof, calling down for them to take care. He waits for the lane to empty and then he picks his paintbrush back up. His feet ache, the insteps curling, and he adjusts his position, his eyes snagging on the tallest of the three minarets with its lopsided smile of a crescent moon. It makes him pause, the brush poised in his hand. He feels something lift inside him, some moment of his soul: a new road is calling. He only has one more job after this one, maybe two more weeks of work, and then he will be on it, that new road. Strange thing is, he doesn't at first see her on the road beside him. Then he remembers. The powder has dried. He swirls the brush inside the colours again and with his mouth a hard line gets back to work.

Once home, he is washing at the stone bath when he feels Mai's approach.

'A word,' she says.

He takes his time, sliding a towel off the line, running it twice over his face, his neck, deliberately putting it back, and only then ducking into her room. She is sitting on a straight chair, waiting.

'I'd hoped this was all over.'

He nods up: carry on.

'Your brother's wife.'

He absorbs the words cleanly, without letting show even a single flicker of fear. And, really, it is not her knowledge of the affair that shocks, but more this public airing of it.

'You've had your fun,' she goes on. 'But now it stops.'

'If it doesn't?'

'If it doesn't, I'll strip the bitch and parade her around myself.'

He sighs, already tired of her drama. 'We both know, if you were going to do that, you'd have done it by now. Won't he let you? Does he say he loves her too much?'

'I wanted to give you a chance. No sense in spreading my shit around the village unduly.'

'A kindness. But we're leaving. You won't try to stop us.'

'What a wonderful way to protect your mother's honour. The mother who has given you everything.'

'Well,' he says, laughing hollowly, 'these things happen.'

The words enrage. She stands. 'I'm filing a statement with the village court tomorrow. Might you attend her stripping? The shaving of her head? I'm sure she'd love to see you there.'

He watches her, weighing the threat, and asks, 'Does he know? You didn't answer.'

'Your father never protected me, either,' she says, almost to herself, as if a memory has ambushed her, but then her face sharpens, all the strings pulled taut. 'When are you leaving? The two of you?'

'Does he know?'

She thinks quickly, calculates. 'It would kill him. Let's spare him that.'

'Yes. Because you never could bear to see him hurt, could you?'

They gaze at one another for a long while, each measuring their own pain against the other's, until Mai looks away and Suraj leaves.

33

'How are you feeling now?' Jeet asks Mehar, in the darkness.

'The same. I'm sorry. I don't know what the matter is.'

'Perhaps I should take you to the doctor.'

'As you wish.'

'It's just so expensive.'

She nods in the dark. 'I'm grateful for your patience with me.'

'You're my wife.'

He closes his hand around her ankle and moves it up her calf in one long motion full of desire. She retracts her leg beyond his reach and hears a low growl, like an animal denied.

'I want to do something for you,' he says. He gives her time to respond, but she doesn't. 'I'm having the house painted and I'd like it to be your favourite colour. What is it?'

'I don't have one.'

'Red? Green?' He waits. 'Pink?'

'Please choose whichever you like.'

He sighs, defeated. 'As you wish.'

Mai catches him leaving the room and he follows her into the barn, away from any ears.

'She was welcoming?' Mai asks.

'She's still not well.'

'Pish. She'll give your brother a child first.'

'Stop. Please.' He paces around the barn, hands on his hips, and Mai lets him stew in his pain a little.

Then, 'I still think the court should know,' she says, testing things out. 'Why not let them sort it?'

'No.' He comes right up to her, finger in her face. 'Don't do that. Don't ever do that.'

'Your brother's not going to give her up.'

'You've spoken to him? What did he tell you?'

'That he's leaving with her, of course.' Mai waits a beat. 'He says he enjoys her too much.'

And it is that word, enjoys, that makes him seethe. 'He doesn't care a thing for her.'

'Hmm. Who's to know?' Mai watches her son, wondering if she needs to goad him more. 'You know, if there's one thing I've learned, it's that there's a man for every occasion. Perhaps you could come to like the thought of your younger brother inside your wife.'

'She's mine,' he snarls. 'She's mine. She's my wife.' His voice breaks and he whispers, as if uttering some blasphemy: 'He's the one who should go.'

She had been waiting for this, but she knows he won't think of it, that he's never been able to see that little bit further. 'Do you mean the revolutionaries? Are they still looking for men?'

He looks across, not sure if this suggestion has come from him or from her.

'It'll take a few days to find them. You could set off in the morning. I'll say you're looking for cattle.'

'He's my brother.'

'Think straight, fool. He probably won't die, but he'll be out of the way. Time enough for you to get your seed in. She'll be yours again.'

34

While Jeet's away and the painters fill the yard, consuming everyone's attention, or so they think, there is opportunity for the lovers to meet spontaneously. Suraj comes up with a sign: a pile of enamel bricks that he stacks in one corner of the barn, under a tent of cut wheat.

When he asks her to take control in their lovemaking, to be on top of him, she blanches, and then the shyness escalates to fear when he asks her again.

'Please,' he adds. 'I'd like it very much.'

She can't look at him; her head is off to the side so her hair hangs like a screen between them. Her hands on his small chest. He is staring at her. Her thighs, either side of his own, burn against his skin. His hands run up to her hips, sleek with sweat, then further up, to her waist with its small pocket of a stomach. He can hear her faint pants behind the curtain of her hair and feels himself contract bodily, exquisitely; she so devastates him it is almost like grief, the knowledge that floods him that he must be with her for ever.

'I want to go,' she says, once dressed, and she feels him nod, his chin tapping several times against the top of her head. 'Why can't we go now? When can we leave?'

'Soon.'

'When?'

'I get paid in a week or so. That shoe store. I think I can get even more out of him.'

'Aren't you clever.'

'No match for you.'

'I mean it, Suraj. I want to go soon.'

He pauses, perhaps because she used his name. What's got into her? 'I said soon.'

'In the meantime, your brother keeps visiting.' She's forcing his hand, she knows.

'There's nothing I can do about that.'

'You can get me away.'

'Money first.'

'You can earn in Lahore.'

'It's a matter of a few days!'

She swallows her riposte, then steps clear of his arms. 'Was my plait tied up?' He juts out his bottom lip – he doesn't remember – and she starts braiding her hair, fingers working anxiously. Straightening back up, she flicks the plait behind her. 'I'm with child,' she says.

Nothing moves on his face and there is a long silence, so long it comes to seem absurd and they both give in to laughter, to giggling really, giggling without being able to stop.

A surprise awaits her at the farm: the decorators have finished preparing the walls, and all four men are stationed evenly along the porch, holding exceedingly long brooms topped with balls of cloth. They are whistling, happily enough, whistling as they daub the house with her very favourite shade of pink.

***

I'd been living at the farm for over a month when I felt ready to leave its gates for the first time and make for the main bazaar. I walked the first kilometre before jumping on a passing tuk-tuk, disembarking in the busy village centre. It was so much louder than I remembered: the chickens, the bartering, the motorbikes and wind chimes, the hymns blaring statically through the temple's rooftop speakers. Above all this commerce, the sky was extravagantly blue, and two distant planes seemed destined to collide, until they didn't, and sailed silently on.

I found the dhaba down a long side lane full of shoe-sellers, and a large woman in a tight apron glanced up from frying dumplings in a giant wok of oil.

'Food all okay?' she asked, before I'd said a word.

'Great. Thank you. But you can stop sending it now.'

'You leaving?'

'I'll cook my own.'

She smiled, slyly, her eyes still on the oil, bubbling hard. 'He's cooking his own food,' she said to the dumplings, and I wondered if they weren't dumplings at all but the severed heads of customers who'd pissed her off. A man sitting at a nearby table belched and grinned.

'Will you be keeping your lady-friend fed?' he asked, and I stepped back quickly, as if stung, nodded a goodbye at the woman and set off towards the main road.

While I was there I got my hair cut, shorter than I'd ever had it before. Then I decided to pop in on my uncle at the bank, if only to show him how much healthier I now was, but he wasn't in, sent out by the manager to buy him a fridge, the guard said and laughed. As I left, I saw Kuku, my aunt, coming up the lane, a burgundy handbag wedged tight under her armpit and Sona struggling to keep up. They walked straight past me, Kuku's face firm and uninterested, but she paused at her house, as though a tiny dart had pierced her back, and turned slowly round.

'Feeling better?' I asked Sona, who nodded, wide-eyed and silent.

'No thanks to you,' Kuku said. I raised my face to meet hers. 'You look well,' she went on, and I swear she seemed affronted by that.

'Much better.'

'I hear you've become fast friends with one of our doctors.'

'It's the talk of the town.'

'Is it just the two of you living there?'

'She doesn't live there. She's done nothing wrong.'

'She visits you? Food and women straight to your door. Haven't you done well this summer?'

'Ask Tanbir Singh if you don't believe us. Instead of giving us a bad name.' Us: part of me was revelling in all this, in being thought of as Radhika's lover, perhaps even hoping that it was in some deep sense true.

'The teacher?' she said, after a pause. She seemed curious. 'What would he know?'

'A lot more than you.'

'I don't doubt it.' Her expression faltered, and something like pain crossed her face. 'Is he with her, the teacher?'

Shaking my head in despair, I walked away. A scandal, that was all these people wanted, some easy story that they could loop around a person's neck, and lynch them with.

Later, at the farm, Radhika, Tanbir and I were all smoking, she fanning herself lazily with the end of her silk scarf, a tangerine thing with red fish scales. Our plates were stacked by the water pump. I'd made a cauliflower and potato curry, the way Tanbir had showed me. Evening light dappled through the plane trees, throwing coins and lines against the wall behind us. Many minutes passed, and then Tanbir flopped back against the wall.

'So, for how much longer are you with us?'

'Couple of weeks,' I replied.

'Same,' Radhika said, and I smiled. 'Back to the clinics of Hyderabad.' She lit another cigarette. 'Do you think you'll come back?' she asked. 'After your studies?'

'Of course I will. I love it here.' Just by saying that word, love, I felt closer to her, and the fact of our leaving within days of each other, as if together, made our time seem fated.

'You love it here?' she repeated.

'I feel at home.'

Slowly she nodded, took a drag on her Marlboro. 'You like being around people who look like you. A sentimental thing.'

'It doesn't feel sentimental. It feels true.'

'But it is sentimental,' Tanbir interjected, in a firm way that irritated me. 'Spend long enough here and you'll fall out of love with it too.'

'Which is also sentimental,' Radhika said.

'We can't all be as itinerant as you,' he replied harshly, which surprised me.

Radhika was smiling around her cigarette. 'Is that why you've stayed here? To allow yourself to fall out of love with the place?'

'You know what the best thing is about falling out of love? It sets you free. Because when you're in love it is everything, it is imprisoning, it is all there is, and you'd do anything, anything, to keep that love. But when it withers you can suddenly see the rest of the world again, everything else floods back into the places that love had monopolised.'

She tapped her ash on to the ground and was gazing at him curiously, steadily. I wanted to say something to her, to add words of my own to the conversation about love, but I couldn't think of any.

'What of your ancestor?' Radhika said then, and gestured to my room. 'I wonder what love did for her.'

Tanbir spoke. 'It's different for women, isn't it? They have no choice in where they go. They grow up in a prison and then get married into one.' He too looked at my room, with its iron bars. 'I mean – Jesus. At least we've moved on from that.'

'Not all prisons have bars,' Radhika said, extinguishing the cigarette under her sandal. 'And not all love is a prison.'

Tanbir lowered his chin on to his chest, as if he was giving this the greatest and most considered thought, but he didn't say anything further. The sun had almost disappeared and by the time the first of the bats made themselves heard, Radhika and Tanbir had left and I had the courtyard to myself again. I wandered over to my room and held its bars. A woman, my great-grandmother, had been locked in here. I remembered Prince mentioning it on that morning when I'd been more concerned what Radhika would make of my food deliveries. How typical, to fixate on the thing that was least important and not hear the thing that mattered. I peered through the bars and imagined Mehar sitting on the other side, and I wondered what her life might have been.

*

A few days later the three of us put the final touches to the house and celebrated with whisky and fried fish that Tanbir bought from the bazaar. We ate on the roof, in what felt to me like the only pool of moonlight in the entire world. Radhika looked stunning. Her eyes gleamed, her smiling teeth rested on her full bottom lip. She'd piled her thick hair back off her face and her long prominent collarbones flared out. When she walked on top of the wall, she didn't seem at all afraid of falling, of the sheer drop to the brown field.

'I think we should buy this place off my uncle and live here,' I said, my voice high with drink.

Some music started up, I've no idea from where, and Radhika and I were dancing, ballroom-style, and I remember my fingers were greasy with all the fish and I apologised whenever they touched her back, her shoulder. She kept laughing and Tanbir watched her with what looked like pride.

'You've had your hair cut!' she said. 'I'm so pleased.'

'Ages ago. I didn't think you'd noticed.'

She twirled out, then back to me, and I wanted to tell her that I thought I loved her, that she was unlike anyone else I'd ever known, but I didn't, or for some reason couldn't.

More drinking and laughter followed, and I can't remember much of what else was said, but I do have a memory of drifting off to sleep and of Radhika pulling a cotton sheet over me, while, at the top of the stairs, Tanbir waited, spinning the keys to his scooter.

When I woke, it took me a moment to blink away the dream-trails and realise I was still on the roof. There was a slight nip in the air so I wrapped the white sheet around me and stepped towards the edge. The morning mist was dove-grey and light and lifting away from the fields. I looked but I could see no child making his unhappy way through them. That child seemed to have gone. What remained was a feeling of quiet rapture, of dawn colours slowly involving themselves with the day, a champagne brightness starting to warm my skin and the waving acres of corn and wheat, the soft green hills that followed no pattern, a distant stone hut that held the horizon and a long tapered track driving on until I couldn't even imagine that I could see it. The orange sun broke upwards and placed, and they did seem placed, great beams of light across all that waiting land. For the first time in my life I had a sense of the world turning. All these years later and I can still see myself standing there, spellbound, marvelling, my breath taken.

35

From the safety of their rooftop, the three women watch the riots over in the main village. Small fires burn. Smoke rises. Gurleen, whose eyesight is sharpest, says she can see men leaping from roof to roof, tin helmets on their heads.

'You can see what's on their heads?' Harbans says dubiously.

'Well. Almost.'

Eventually, Mai informs them that things have calmed down, that the village court has managed to clamp down on the ringleaders and call a truce. God knows how long it will last.

'But who was fighting?' Mehar asks. 'Was it about that whole dominion business?'

'Well, I'm blown!' Gurleen says, snorts. 'What fancy ways she now talks!'

It is Suraj who tells her that for once the British weren't involved, not directly, at any rate; that the Hindus and the Sikhs had tried to create a Mohammedan-only quarter of the village outside which they weren't to stray, and the Mussulmans had retaliated by smashing the statue of Krishna above the sweetshop.

'It's no longer there?' Mehar says, incredulous. 'Lord Krishna's statue?'

'I wish you wouldn't say "Lord". It's painted stone.'

'It's what it represents. And I'll say what I like.'

He reminds himself that she is barely sixteen. The impertinence will go. 'I noticed the guavas were especially fine today,' he says, brightening, and he takes one from her basket, sits up and starts gobbling it gleefully.

'Such a child,' she says. 'I don't know anyone who loves them as much as you.'

'Have some. You need to be eating more now.'

She shakes her head. 'Too sweet.'

'For the baby, then. Don't let him miss out.'

Before she leaves, he says she shouldn't go too close to the village, where things are still jittery, and should take the circling route via the rear cornfield instead. It near doubles her walk home and the path is full of dung and dense with wasps, so many wasps that she has to lower her arms and bring them under the protection of her veil. She can feel their little legs on her nose, her ears, a shifting mass pressing through the material, as if searching for a way to her face. She is cowering, absolutely frightened, but knows she can only carry on. What must she look like, a walking cloak of wasps? She should ask Gurleen for mint when she gets home. Even once she is free of them all, she can still feel them covering her, hear their frantic drilling.

36

It is dawn and already Mai is sitting up, cursing the light, groping about under her charpoy for sandals. Everyone covers their feet first. You never know when a scorpion might get caught underfoot, though Mai is rumoured to have crushed a baby one with her naked heel. She stretches high and fully, arching her back, and it is only when she brings her arms down that she spots Jeet out in the yard, gazing at the new pink wall.

'Had breakfast?' she asks, yawning. She traps a fly against her neck, examines it, then dusts the sparkly remains to the ground.

'I've not been back an hour.'

'Did you find them?'

He nods, still admiring the house.

'You have his details? Telegram? It shouldn't take them long to get here?'

He says nothing for a while, and then: 'Did she like it? The colour? Has she said anything? She does like it, doesn't she?'

'Oh, you poor thing,' Mai says, running a hand down the length of Jeet's arm, and he puts his head against her shoulder and breaks down in tears.

That night, he asks for Mehar and she is waiting on the bed when he arrives, though he doesn't cross the room. Instead, he says into the blackness, 'Are you here?'

'Yes,' she replies, and waits for him to come, ready to flinch from his touch and beg forgiveness for still being unwell. But she doesn't hear him move from the door.

'I only wanted to check how you were.'

'No improvement yet. I'm very sorry.'

'Don't be. But I'm back now and promise to look after you better.'

Her hand goes to her stomach and the child growing inside, and something like pity for her husband flows through her. 'I hope it was a successful trip? Did you find good cattle?'

'Yes, thank you. Whatever success means. Time will tell.'

She hears something, a rattle, his hand on the doorknob.

'I'll let you rest,' he says, and he leaves her lying there in the deep dark, still stroking her stomach.

37

Determined to find the men, Jeet had hung around the city temple morning, noon and night, making enquiries, offering bribes, until at last he caught the necessary lead and was handed an address. He went the next day, surprised to discover not a dark, secret hideaway, but a house like any other: small, clean, a leather settee and wide rosewood bed, just off the main thoroughfare in Jalandhar. Maybe they weren't hiding at all.

'It's my sister's place,' Tegh Singh explained, as teas arrived. 'They're keeping an eye on things in Delhi. Never know when that pandit might screw us over.'

Jeet nodded. He was sitting on the very lip of the settee, puzzled at the opulence of a table made of glass, at the workings of the cloth fan mounted overhead. There were several other men waiting around the edge of the bed, quiet, solemn, no doubt keen to hear the reason behind Jeet's visit. A map of India hung across the wall, inset with a more detailed one of Punjab.

'You came to our house,' Jeet began. 'We contributed money to your fight. Our fight,' he adjusted.

'Yes, of course. Your mother.'

'Yes.' Jeet sipped his tea. 'Are you still planning the attack? In Delhi?'

'You've come to join? We still need men. Brave men.'

'Will the men survive, do you think?'

Tegh Singh leaned forward over the table, and Jeet saw the pistol at his back. 'It's a fight for freedom. There will be casualties. But,' he went on, reclining, 'you'll die with your head high, I promise you that. Songs will be sung about you.'

Suraj was right, Jeet thought. He really was a fool, this Tegh Singh, a worthy and humourless one. Despite his shaking hand, Jeet put his cup down so carefully it didn't make a sound on the glass. 'Not me. My brother. You may come and take him when the time is right.'

38

Lakhpatti Shoewear has a huge awning and into its shade Suraj pulls his cart and begins arranging his stencils and pots: the powder, the water, the flour and the salt. His brushes are clean and he runs his thumb over the bristles of each one before lining them all up. Around him the lane is greasy with sun. Three shirtless boys are baiting a starving dog. A pastry-seller sets himself up on the corner, oil spitting from his shallow pan. Veiled women lean over tiny balconies, whispering, pointing out things below: the escaped hog, the old teacher dyeing his beard, the two white men jumping the queue at the soda cart. The balconies and the arched windows and, behind all the fancy brickwork, the sleeping courtesans, dreaming gravely until the mistress shocks them with a jug of thrown water and the morning chores begin. All the while, over the bazaar, beyond the mosque, the sun continues to rise, indifferent to it all. He does love being in a city.

When he's finished the second coat and just about succeeded in drawing the strap of a sandal so it curls around the length of the 'k', the proprietor appears, lips glistening with syrup.

'Looking nice, Mr Painter. Looking nice.'

'It's even better than I thought,' Suraj says, descending the ladder. He keeps one foot on the lowermost rung to suggest an eagerness to get back on it and do a good job. 'Shall I add a gold surround?'

'A gold surround? Do I look like I piss money?'

'It's in season, uncle. And no one else has it. Your friend has only a bronze.'

The proprietor turns towards The Shoe King across the avenue, with its brown board filled with insistent capital letters. No image at all, of a sandal or a shoe, or even a crown. Some king!

'He came nosing around yesterday,' Suraj says. 'Asking what I was up to.'

'He did? Go for gold. All around, yes.'

'It'll be the best sign in the bazaar. Have no fear.' The owner cuts his eyes, because it is clear this is a claim too large. 'You can pay me when I'm finished,' Suraj says.

'Finish first, yes?'

'Three days and I'll be done. Pay me in full. I don't want to have to come all the way back to collect the money. Three days.'

Home by late afternoon, he goes first to douse his head at the pump, strangling the rubber seal to keep the water from fountaining everywhere. When he stands up, it is straight into Jeet's gaze.

'You're back,' Jeet says.

'Seems so.'

'You left early this morning.'

'I had to fetch my cart.'

Jeet nods: of course, the cart. 'There's a rumour wheat prices have gone up. Thought I'd go now and check it out.' He points to the bicycle by the gate. 'Come with me. We'll double-saddle. Like we used to.'

'No. Thank you. I'm tired. I'm going to rest.'

'I should have thought. You rest.' He places his hand on his youngest brother's shoulder and for a moment Suraj thinks he sees emotion in his eyes. 'I do care about you, you should know that. I care that you're working so hard. Don't you get scared,' he goes on, taking back his hand, 'that high up the ladder?'

'A little, at first. Not so much now.'

Jeet smiles, turns away, and Suraj watches him ride off, feeling as if something true has passed between them, to do with the pain of being brothers in this place. Sighing, he sits on the warm edge of the stone bath and is glad of the unexpected peace, of the opportunity to get a good and proper look at the farm. He won't miss it, he is sure, with its smallness and boredom, the way it throttles life.

He'll be glad to go, though once they are away and all this adventure is over and he has her to himself, will that be enough? Will she be enough? Will he be a good father to his boy? He shakes the thought free. Leave that for later. First he needs to speak to her. He stands and peels his trousers from his skin, where the wetness of the ledge has seeped through. He looks over to the window, slatted shut, and imagines her lying inside, in the dark, out of the heat ... Though that is not where she is.

At that moment, Mehar and her sisters-in-law are in the enclosure at the rear of the farm, planting a peepal tree in the upper right corner of the walled pen. Why they're planting this tree with its heart-shaped flowers, Mehar doesn't know. It is simply something that Mai has ordered them to do.

'You do it,' Gurleen says, and thrusts the clay pot at Mehar. 'Please,' she adds, with rank insincerity.

'Oh, for pity's sake, can't you even ... ?' But why argue? If she gets this over with, she can start frying the snacks she plans to take for the journey. Something to share and nibble on the way to Lahore. So she crouches and Harbans passes her a trowel and soon a hole has been dug and she removes the baby peepal from its clay basin and presses it into the peat. Done, she squints up into the faces of her sisters-in-law, which are violently framed by the sun. 'Water?' But neither has brought any and neither looks like budging so Mehar rises to her feet in a show of frustration and is through the barn when she sees Suraj idling by the gate, hands on his slim hips. She pauses, watches him. What is it that is making him smile? What is he thinking of? Where is his fear? She pulls her veil down and continues across the yard, towards the pump, where she takes up a brass jug. She can feel him approach, darkening the light over that side of her veil.

'I can do that,' he says, so she leaves the jug on the ground and steps back. He bends into her field of vision and runs his fingers over the jug's rim. 'Be ready to leave in three days. I'll be waiting at the hut, on horseback. Don't laugh.'

But she is not laughing. She is not even close to laughing. 'If they catch me—'

'They're not going to catch us.' He starts pumping water into the jug, as if to wash away that thought, which he is annoyed she's even brought up. 'They won't catch us.' He remembers the stars, and that he and Mehar are forging something new. 'There's enough meaning in the world to allow us that at least.'

She says she should go, that they'll wonder what's taking her so long, and he passes up the jug full of water.

'Next time you speak to me I'll be on a horse!' Is it levity he is attempting? She's not sure and a note of doubt plays suddenly loud in her mind: is he serious? Is it a game? She turns and steps back through the barn, feeling light-headed, dizzy. She halts, takes a sip of the water, then continues out, where the sisters-in-law are still standing around the peepal. Mehar pours, muttering a prayer as the soil soaks and darkens.

39

In three days. Those words, like the sun's incessant eye, follow her everywhere around the farm. At the pump, folding two curd spoons into the end of her chunni. On the roof, where she rolls her underwear into one tight ball and secures it with string. In the barn, on her knees, petitioning God. By the final evening, a bag is loaded and hidden in the field and she is clear in her mind where she must be and at what hour. But she wants her shawl, the one her family gave to her, and so she slips into Mai's room, takes it from the cupboard, and then folds it into an old salwar and hides it in the china room.

***

I didn't wait for the tuk-tuk to come to a complete stop before I jumped out and headed to the surgery. I'd been thinking about us all night and was finally ready to tell Radhika how I felt. I figured she'd probably already guessed at my feelings for her, but I worried that she thought me too young, too immature for anything serious to develop between us. I wanted to sit her down and calmly tell her I wasn't. When I arrived, though, Dr Duggal said she was out doing her rounds.

'For all the good she does,' he sneered.

'Will she back soon?'

He shrugged. 'You look healthier,' he told me. 'So it was dengue. Like I said.'

I waited for her at a drinks stand opposite, until Prince spotted me and said he'd seen Radhika boarding the city bus. Perhaps he clocked the disappointment on my face because he called me over to where he was sitting with some friends and dealt me into their game of cards. They taught me how to play *bhabhi*, which was brand new to me then but a game I can still play.

'He's staying at that farm,' Prince said, and the other boys nodded, because clearly this was not news to them. 'In the locked room,' he went on, darkly.

However curious I was about life again, and especially about that room and Mehar, I knew Prince wasn't the person to ask. I resolved quietly to broach it again with Tanbir when we next met. I stood up.

'One more game?' Prince suggested, but I said goodbye and started for home, which felt such a long way now that I'd missed seeing Radhika.

The following morning, I was reading my book on the roof when I heard a bicycle clatter into the yard. I felt my heart lift – had someone told her I was looking for her? – but from the top of the stairs I saw that it was only Jai, my uncle, yanking up the cotton of his bottoms and climbing clumsily off. He waited for me to come all the way down before turning from the house and towards me.

'It looks like new,' he said. 'So do you,' he added.

'I had help,' I said, and he nodded, carefully, as if help wasn't the word he'd use to describe what had been going on here.

'I'm sorry I've not been to see you. Things got busy at work and then Sona got a cough.' The mention of a cough seemed to require a clearing of his own throat. 'I con-firmed your return flight.' He passed me my inky plane tickets, which were stapled at one end like a raffle book. 'A week today. I'm working but you can get an auto to the city coach stand and ... Well, I'm sure you'll be fine.' He kicked up the lever holding up his bike and swung back on to the saddle.

When I tried to thank him, he said angrily, 'I don't think there's any need for you to be entertaining that man in my house again. What a fine way you have of repaying my hospitality.'

He left after that, and I couldn't stop myself from walking out of the gate and along the dirt track, agitated, past the rear pen and towards Sunra, Tanbir's village.

Though I'd started leaving the farm more often, to talk to passers-by, to buy food in the market, it was the first time I'd gone this way. At the village gate I chose a lane that ran between two building sites and found myself at a choleric swamp, full of corrugated tin and a half-submerged plaster cast of a four-armed Shiva. Cows drank sadly on the far side, wasps hovered in torrid black clouds, and the stench of shit and gas rose off the stagnant water. I made my way round it, the cows lifting their big heads and eyeing my every step, and then turned down a long ribbon of a track, two brown grooves and a shaved line of yellowed grass running up the middle, like a landing strip for birds. I found that the track circled around the village, with flat-roofed houses to one side and a vast cornfield on my right. Since Tanbir wasn't expecting me, I wasn't in any hurry; I even enjoyed being lost for a while, and felt a stab of indignation when a voice called out to me from a nearby roof: 'Come up, come up.' The old man looked familiar, I thought, as I approached his house. It was a confined place, dark, with a dry gutter running along its empty doorway, and I had to duck all the way up the stairs.

'I hear you've been playing cards.' Now I knew him – it was Laxman, only topless, wearing a white sheet as a sarong, his chest creased like an accordion.

'He's a bit of a shark, your Prince.'

'He didn't get his visa. We'll have to think of something else.'

I said I was sorry. 'It's not easy these days.'

'Not for some of us, no.'

Humbled, I looked to the cornfield and asked if it was his. He laughed at the mere idea and said that, no, the parrot farm belonged to a family who'd long emigrated to Surrey, in Canada.

'Are there parrots?' I asked, looking to the sky, as if the birds might magically appear.

'Talk sense. The old fart who originally bought it simply had a massive nose.' Laxman shrugged, as if to say such was the stupidity of man. 'He's long dead but the name's always stuck. See that hut way over there? I actually thought that's where you were going. The Lovers' Hut.'

He was gesturing over my shoulder. I looked and in the distance I saw a small shack of yellow brick.

'Why's it called that?'

He hesitated. 'I wouldn't want to speak out of turn about your ancestor.'

'Mehar Kaur? Can you tell me something about her? I'd like to know.'

'It's just old rumour,' he said. 'She strayed with a brother. He went away and left her behind.' Carefully, he folded away a towel drying on the wall. 'Who knows, though, really?'

'He left her?'

'So they say. Hit the road and never came back. Though I also heard he died and their mother buried his ashes under a peepal tree.' He grinned gummily. 'The tales we tell!'

'And she was locked in that room?'

'Who knows?' he said again. 'Who's here to tell her story?'

I nodded silently, wondering how much of this was true, or if that was even the right question, but nevertheless feeling a kind of despair for this woman, my great-grandmother, whom I'd never known.

'Anyway,' he said, 'what brings you to our small village? A little sleepy for you, no?'

I looked at him. 'Where does the teacher live? Tanbirji?'

He walked me over to the other side of his roof and described a long diagonal over the houses, all the way to a vast black Airtel satellite dish. 'See the red building next to it? That's your aunt's old house. The teacher lives in the lane behind.'

He said it would be easiest for me to just hop from house to house, keeping the dish in view, so I did, charting a wayward path over the roofs, jumping, climbing, ducking under washing lines, treading warily across old bridges arching over cobbled lanes. I asked permission from the few people I encountered, but no one seemed to care. When I reached the satellite dish, it looked so out of place that I imagined its face scanning the skies for some sign of its real home.

My aunt's old house looked like it hadn't been lived in for years: the window fogged, door sealed. I moved to the edge of the flat roof, looking for signs of Tanbir. It took me a little while to locate his scooter, which was parked inside his house, directly behind my aunt's. They would have grown up together. My mind started to race. My uncle's words that first night: *a neighbour from her own village.* I thought of Tanbir's repeated questions about her; of the time I'd seen her at the bank, her pain. *Is he with her, the teacher?*

Swallowing, I leaned out for a wider view into his courtyard, where there was a small square table with many books piled on it. And there it was, on one of the three chairs, Radhika's scarf, with the fish-scale pattern. My gaze dropped to the lane below, to the gunny sack hanging over Tanbir's doorway and, poking out of the sack, the wheel of Radhika's bike. I felt grief, confusion too at how blind I'd been. Tears threatened, though they remained as a heavy sensation behind my eyes. But then the gunny sack was held aside, Radhika stepped out, and feeling I'd been caught spying, I turned away and ran back across the roofs.

Afterwards, I hoped she'd come by so I could explain, but she didn't, and suddenly I only had a few days left. Desperate to do something, I went to the bazaar one morning to buy books – her idea – when the barber called out to me: 'Jai's nephew!'

I looked over the road, but it was the customer who spoke, through the face foam. 'Your doctor-lady's looking for you.'

Apprehensively, I stopped off at the surgery, where Radhika was folding an Anglepoise lamp into a box full of grey textbooks. Tanbir's scooter was outside, but I couldn't see him.

Her face softened as she set down the lamp. She took a step and placed her arms around me, holding me close. I put my arms around her, too, but uncertainly, my hands barely brushing her shirt, as though the feelings borne by that embrace were extraordinarily fragile.

'You're leaving now?' I said.

'They need me back sooner. Staff shortage,' she added, returning to her boxes. 'You should see old man Duggal. Jumping for joy.'

'But – now?'

She sighed. 'I'm leaving.'

I tried to thank her in a roundabout, clumsy way, unable once again to say the things I wanted, though perhaps also learning that we don't always need to, and then Tanbir entered, acknowledging me with a nod. He handed Radhika a bottle of water.

'Thank you,' she said softly, and he nodded again.

Were they in love? Did he ask her to stay? Did she want him to leave with her? I never knew.

Radhika looked down at her hands, made some tiny adjustments to the way her skirt was draped over her knees, and then raised her face and smiled at me. She lifted the cardboard box.

'Can I carry that for you?' Tanbir asked, though he took no step towards her, and wasn't meeting her eye.

'Don't worry,' she said. 'It's not heavy.'

I'd leave, too, before the end of the week, but not before my aunt Kuku surprised me by turning up at the farm to say goodbye. I was pegging out my final load of washing, I remember; my suitcase lay open behind me.

'So I hear she's gone, your doctor-friend.' She looked pleased, but in a brittle way.

'Her work finished,' I said.

'No more parties for you, then. For you and her and that teacher.'

'I guess not.'

'I expect you were both sad to see her go?'

I put my empty basket by the entrance to my room and turned to face her properly. There was something formidable in the way she was bracing herself, this woman who'd not been permitted to marry the boy from her village, who had instead been forced into a loveless marriage with my uncle while Tanbir carried on affairs with whomever he wanted. He had moved on and out of love with her. She had never been allowed the means to do the same.

'I was sad,' I told Kuku. 'I don't know about the teacher.'

'I'm sure they were all over each other. Dogs in heat.'

A hot breeze sent up some courtyard dust and I wondered if falling out of love was different to letting go of the pain. I made a decision: I wanted to protect us both. 'I'd be surprised,' I said.

'No?' She paused, then asked quickly, 'Were they not close?'

'Not to my knowledge, no.'

I don't know whether she believed me. I don't think she did; possibly she also resented my attempt to spare her.

'Can I ask you something?' I said, looking across to my room. 'Do you ever think of my great-grandmother? Do you know anything about her?'

She looked at the room, too, though all she said was, 'I knew the hut.'

Up on the roof, I watched her heading back towards home, pushing away the track, away from Sunra with every step. The giant new statue of Krishna loomed above her. He was playing a flute, after all, just as Radhika had wanted, and in that moment, with all that sky in front of me, I glimpsed a future and was overcome by a sudden feeling that things would be different from here on in, that I would never use again, that I would go to London, make friends, have lovers and forge a life of my own choosing. Now, twenty years on, I smile to think of him, to remember the eighteen-year-old who didn't appreciate how things resurface, who couldn't know that he would relapse twice, recover twice, that the underlying hurt does not go away and can only be paid attention to. When the taxi bleats its horn and he zips his suitcase and stands it on the ground, there is the poignancy of farewell in the air, and it is perhaps this that makes him feel he is being watched as he leaves the room and crosses the courtyard. He even turns round at the gate and half-expects to see someone standing at the window. There is no one there, of course, just an offcut of red bunting, blown in from somewhere and floating free along the roof.

40

On the day of their flight, Suraj arrives at the stud farm and the horse he chooses matches exactly his ideal. It is a full-tilt mahogany beast, with a noble white kite along the broad length of its face and hot breath streaming from its nostrils. He runs his hand repeatedly over the dip in the animal's back, and says something into the pink folds of its ear. Turning round, he whistles across to the owner.

'We're having problems with roamers around our wells. Am I okay to do a quick raid around our fields tonight? I'll have it back to you in the morning.'

The man, stout and with thick, tussocky sideburns, his moss-green tunic straining over his gut, walks with such short steps that Suraj figures his back must be hurting. 'This one?' he pants, arriving at his side after what feels like a month.

'He's perfect.'

'Sure you can handle him?'

'Two okay?'

'Make it ten.'

'Ten!' But this is no time to haggle. The horse will be his. He takes another three coins from his breast pocket and hands them over. 'Daylight robbery,' he says, unable to resist.

'There's millet and brown seed,' the owner says, indicating the saddlebags lumped either side of the horse. 'Freshly ground. I don't want him fed any old shit.'

'You've nothing to worry about, uncle. I'll take better than better care of him.'

As he takes the reins and leads the horse away, Suraj noses the animal's soft brown bristles. 'Fly fast for me, won't you?' he murmurs. The owner, hands on his waist, is still watching when they arrive at the field's edge. 'You must be his fucking lover,' Suraj mutters, as he mounts and feels an instant wave of power, of command, and urges the horse into a trot.

Once at the hut, Suraj jumps off, and steers the animal round to the back, away from Sunra's village gate. He kisses its coat and the horse lowers its head into its short shadow and starts to graze.

He moves to the doorway; the brown satchel is inside, full of his earnings. The shoe-seller had even tipped generously, overjoyed with his finished sign. He has enough now to set them up with a room until he can find work.

Surely even in Lahore they'll need sign painters? Suraj looks over to the horse, who turns shyly towards a fresh patch of grass, and then he lifts his gaze to the more distant village beyond. His Kala Sanghian. He has thought about heading to the farm for a final look at the place, but has decided that is sentimental, and that what he wants more than anything is never to see any of it again. Not the barn, not the shit, not those flat roofs and bell-ringing temples, not the white cupola of the single gurdwara. They will make a new life in Lahore, he and Mehar. He gains clarity in this moment, as he stands at the doorway waiting for nightfall, wondering if she'll come. On the cusp of leaving, he is shaken to realise that he doesn't want to do any of this without her, that he is, and much more than he'd allowed for, helplessly in love.

Hours later, the middle of the night, and Mehar hears the gate being unlocked. She sits up at the window to see Jeet cycling away. Trouble at the wells again, perhaps. Swinging her feet round, she presses them into her wooden slippers. She is not as nervous as she had expected to be: her fear seems to have dried up, hardened into a more forceful thing, some instrument of coercion pushing her on. At least they are the best slippers, she thinks. The least splintered. Likely to survive a long journey. Not often she gets to wear them, these best ones. And they fit. Maybe she is nervous after all. Holding her breath, she wraps the shawl around herself and stands up.

'Who is it?'

She isn't immediately sure whether that's Harbans or Gurleen. 'Me. Go back to sleep. It's not morning yet.'

'You need to soo-soo?' It is Harbans, and Mehar hears concern in her voice, and then the sound of her sitting up.

'I'll be quick. Stay.'

'Don't be silly. With all this trouble about?'

Mehar doesn't insist, doesn't want to raise suspicions, and they make it all the way to the water pump before Mai steps out from under the porch and asks them where they think they're going.

'To make use of the field,' Mehar says, determining to now go via the road, that she can't risk Mai catching her doubling back on to the track.

'Both of you? It's not a night for walks.'

'But it's so dark,' Harbans says.

'I wouldn't want to lose you both, then, would I? Harbans, you go back to sleep. I'll wait here for her.'

Harbans looks puzzled, reluctant to obey, until Mehar says, 'Don't worry,' and touches her arm in a warm gesture she hopes Harbans might later recall. When they ask who was the last to see Mehar, it will be Harbans who answers. This thought came to Mehar as they left their room, and it's one that pleases her. Harbans has always been the kindest of the women.

In a wave of feeling, Mehar takes off her wedding shawl, which Harbans had loved at first sight, and passes it to her. 'I thought it'd be colder,' she says, by way of explanation. Then Mehar glances at Mai, but the older woman doesn't speak. Perhaps she is standing too far away to see.

'I won't be long,' Mehar tells them, and steps into the wheat, continuing until she arrives at the head-high reeds. Her heart feels as vast as the moon that shines over the crops, so low she thinks that with a few more steps she could walk right through it. The stars are scattered across the sky. Scudding clouds. A ragged night. Listening carefully, she kneels and finds the jute bag she's been adding clothes to, hers and his, for the last few days. She whips a drawstring from one of her salwars and ties the bag to her back, covering it with the trail of her chunni.

Now she tunnels forward, head low, parting the stems. She mouths a silent prayer and her step quickens and she bunches the hem of her tunic into a fist to stop it snagging. Stones press into her feet. Red pebbles. Brittle shells. Don't think. Don't. To the road. To the road and then to him, waiting for her on his horse. (Almost: he is crouched on top of the hut, scouting the fields for movement, for her movement. Below him, the horse sleeps, still and dreaming.) The grass shortens, her cover is gone, the moon casts wide its careless light and she registers a feeling of exposure, of coming up for air, but her quick feet trample the thought before she can do anything with it, and then her foot touches warm tar and her veil is sliding off her head and she runs up the road, halving the ground with her feet, climbing into the night, drinking it into her lungs. She heads left, panting, cutting a long and fast diagonal until she nears the neighbouring

village. Slick cobbles flick by, the lanes edged with dai-
sies, petals closed, as if shutting their eyes. She keeps to
the sides, where the darkness is thickest, and at last she
is crossing the track, through the final field of chest-deep
grass, elbowing away the scratch and prickle and closing
in on him, he who is suddenly aware of a river cutting
through the field, breaking towards him, and he jumps
down from the roof and races to meet her and pull her
to the hut.

'You were so long. It'll be light soon.'

She seems not quite able to grant that she's done it,
made it, and as they prepare to set off she wonders if
there's something she ought to be telling him, something
she's missed perhaps, or something she saw in Mai's atti-
tude, in the ease with which she has escaped. It feels as if
she is withholding a crucial detail, one she can't quite let
herself glimpse, a feeling she doesn't want to, can't bear
to, interrogate. Her hand goes to her belly. She only wants
to be away from here. Calmly, he takes the jute sack of
clothes and ties it to the horse's saddlebags.

'We'll cross the field and be out through the far gate.'

'Mai's waiting for me. I had to tell her I needed the
field. We should avoid the outer road.'

'We will, we will.'

'And we should be quiet.'

'Really? And I was hoping we might get my drum out.'

She smiles and he is unfolding his shawl when he asks
about hers, and then gives her his own, which she wears
like a cloak, across her head and face so only her eyes are

visible. Ready, he helps her up on to the horse, feeling how light she is, surprised by it, so light that he overdoes it and hears her laugh, gripping the animal to stop herself from toppling over the other side. He swings himself up in front of her. Her slender arms are around his waist. Her heart thriving against his back. He thinks of their child, of the three of them, their three heartbeats.

'I'm sad for my sisters. I hope they can forgive us.'

She feels his nod and then the jerk of his body as he instructs the horse on – the hooves clanging loud. A verse comes to Mehar, an old sad wedding lament: *The stars have no pity, the mother's helpless foal, the verandas sag with weeping, and girls leave their home.*

'Here,' he says, passing back a hipflask. The rubber bung comes out with a pop and she lifts the flask to her mouth, but it is filled to the brim and the water spills down her chin and on to the horse, darkening its coat. She wipes her mouth dry and runs her fingers through the spillage, creating soft little furrows in the horse's back. Delicate little furrows, she thinks, miniatures of the path they are describing.

There is a lulling quality to their movement through the grass: the high arching walk of the horse, its long grave head. With each step, they rise and fall against each other, a single butting wave. The animal's black eyes seem to contain the night; perhaps the universe entire is in those two gleaming ovals guiding Mehar and Suraj through the old field. They see a large white mouse standing on its hind legs, gnawing excitedly at some secret thing. Nearby a snake lazily uncoils itself and powers off with a boastful whip of its tail, as if it knows the passing strangers are watching. There's a further delight when the cloud cover reveals a moonlit pangolin, snouting away in the soil. It looks up at them, monitoring the lovers' progress as nothing more than foreign scents in the familiar world of its night. All these animals, like spirits at the threshold of a new existence, and not for the first time Mehar imagines a tiny farm outside a small village yarded with a square of neem trees. One buffalo at first. Even that will be a stretch. But, in time, more animals, more children. Perhaps a larger plot of land. Nothing too much. They wouldn't need much. She can make their charpoys. That much she's learned. And her sewing is getting better. The wheat whispers and seeds carry on the surface of the air, falling where they will. Shadows menace and comfort in line with the shifting clouds. From somewhere behind comes the happy skreel of an owl and Mehar wonders if the owl got to the mouse before the snake did. Yes, her sewing is definitely getting better. She should start on mittens and hats, for it'll be midwinter by the time he is born. She is certain it will be a he. The sky pulses on and matter goes about its impersonal business: planets collide, galaxies unravel, black holes the size of a dozen suns swirl with such phenomenal violence that the effect will be registered in millions of years and, yes, mittens first, and she lowers the flask from her lips and forces back in the bung.

At the field's edge there is a long swinging wooden gate kept to with a loop of grey rope. Suraj dismounts, feet flattening the mud, and tramps over, lifting the rope away and pulling the gate wide open as if he were dragging a cow across the field. He looks over to Mehar, into her eyes, which are radiant, soft, but suddenly baffled and afraid and he's about to ask what the matter is when he's tackled to the ground and held there by two men with rifles across their backs. He can't think, tries to scream, but they kick mud into his face, then drag him up on to his feet so all the breath is knocked out of him. Blinking, spitting, he sees wagging lights, torchbearers emerging through the trees, the flames fierce in the coming dawn. The crowd swells and gathers and the men are still at his arms, their nails in his pits.

A woman – Harbans, he thinks, by her gait – helps Mehar off the horse and holds her face. He sees Mai there, too, and then his brothers. But the first to speak is Tegh Singh, the man with the Italian moustache, his beard thickened to little tufts sprouting over his cheeks. Not five years older than Suraj and still with a lot to prove.

'He's ours?'

Mai steps forward and in a clear voice says, 'You can take him.'

Suraj twists violently, but is punched back. Spits of rain appear in the breeze and creep under Mehar's shawl, which is his shawl and full of his smell. She feels the drops cluster on her upper lip, feels them and lets them lie there, under his shawl, untouched and unbroken.

'And what about this sister,' Tegh Singh says. 'His wife?'

'Mine,' says Jeet, coming forward, leaving his bicycle on the ground. He avoids looking at Suraj. 'When we learned that he was trying to run tonight, I sent her to talk to him. I thought he might listen to her. I didn't imagine he'd try to take her with him.'

Tegh Singh looks doubtful. 'True?' he asks Suraj, and the two men holding him draw his arms back tighter, and tighter still, until the boy speaks.

'I want to speak to my brother,' Suraj says, seething.

Tegh Singh turns to Mehar: 'Was he taking you by force, sister? Or were you willing?'

What can she say? Her eyes seek out Suraj, but he is resolutely not looking at her, and in that deliberate avoiding of her gaze she already senses his withdrawal, and in his withdrawal, her stupidity.

'You wouldn't be the first woman to change husbands,' Tegh Singh says.

'Don't shame me,' Jeet says, a threatening edge to his voice. 'I've given you a man. Take him.' Then, more to Suraj: 'If he dies then it'll be an honourable death. I promise him that.'

Tegh Singh approaches – 'Absconding! Taking a woman by force!' – and then he leans in so close that Suraj can feel his breath and the pores in his nose appear to crawl. He speaks in a voice low and intimate. 'I hope she was worth it, because they've got you by the balls.'

'Mai!' Suraj says, straining to look past the young leader.

'You've said enough,' she tells Singh. Then, glaring at Suraj, ensuring he recalls it: 'These things happen.'

*

A week later, against a sky so pristine it hurts her eyes, Mehar will be inside the china room, watching Jeet snap away the black lacquered slats and replace them with iron bars. He will give no reason for doing this and Mehar will not ask. She will silently follow him grout the ledge with quicklime, measure and saw the bars, and then she will count the bars going up, one by one, hammering into the mortar, sealing her in.

She will not know that earlier that same day Jeet had visited Suraj inside his cell and passed him a copy of the holy gutka. 'I hear you leave for Delhi tomorrow. I'll say a prayer for you tonight.'

'If I survive, shall I come back?' Suraj asked him.

'I wouldn't advise it. But it's still your soil.'

'Is it still my child?'

'That's for you to think carefully about,' Jeet replied, and Suraj snorted, said that one way or another he'd be free, and told his brother to leave him.

From this point, as is their habit, the years will spool on. Harbans will have girls followed at last by a boy, and a new husband will take Gurleen to a suburb by the city, where she'll bully the maid and never speak of her first marriage. She will not return for Mai's funeral, by which time Mehar's eldest child will be married and with a young daughter of his own, a daughter who at sixteen is engaged to a quiet boy in England, where together they'll build a life for themselves and for me. There is richness to come, but for Mehar the farm is forever haunted by Suraj's absence. Is he alive or not? Nearby or not? Jeet, thinking it for the best, will tell Mehar nothing of his visit to Suraj in his cell, nor of his brother's words, not when he holds her hand and she recoils from his touch, and not when, after several decades and six children (his brother's, five more), he is suffering a miserably slow death and she continues to withhold her affection. For the rest of her life he lets her believe about his brother whatever it is she needs to believe. Such are the burdens of victory. But for now ...

The day has blued lightly over and birdsong thrills the air. The revolutionaries depart, pulling Suraj with them, and as she watches them go Mai nods once, to herself, and then glances at Gurleen, who looks sharply away, battling tears. The crowd disbands, muttering, and Mehar sees Jeet staring at her, his eyes unreadable, and then he gazes down, at the churned mud. He doesn't move until Mohan squeezes his shoulder and says they should get back too. They are all leaving – how can they be leaving? thinks Mehar, feeling unsteady, and she reaches for Harbans. There, there, Harbans says, it's all over, let's say no more, and cradling Mehar's head against her bosom, she leads her through the gate and out, so that behind them all that remains is the horse, marvellously oblivious, chewing its damp grass at the edge of a farmer's field.